CALL ME RANDY

The Cowboy Tales of Randall J. Jackson

authorHOUSE®

AuthorHouse™ UK Ltd.
500 Avebury Boulevard
Central Milton Keynes, MK9 2BE
www.authorhouse.co.uk
Phone: 08001974150

This book is a work of fiction. People, places, events, and situations are the product of the author's imagination. Any resemblance to actual persons, living or dead, or historical events, is purely coincidental.

©2011. Stuart L. Groom. All rights reserved

No part of this book may be reproduced, stored in a retrieval system, or transmitted by any means without the written permission of the author.

First published by AuthorHouse   04/29/2011

ISBN: 978-1-4567-7334-2

Illustrations by: Jessica Windhorst
Further examples of her artwork can be viewed at:
http://macaosstiefel.deviantart.com/gallery/
email: macaobyjessi@googlemail.com

Any people depicted in stock imagery provided by Thinkstock are models, and such images are being used for illustrative purposes only.
Certain stock imagery © Thinkstock.

AuthorHouse Book Ordering Dept: (0800) 197-4150 UK
AuthorHouse Book Ordering Dept: (888) 280-7715 USA

Website Book Shop UK: www.authorhouse.co.uk
Website Bookstore USA: www.authorhouse.com

This book is printed on acid-free paper.

Because of the dynamic nature of the Internet, any Web addresses or links contained in this book may have changed since publication and may no longer be valid. The views expressed in this work are solely those of the author and do not necessarily reflect the views of the publisher, and the publisher hereby disclaims any responsibility for them.

This publication has been sponsored by Sneezy-Snout Inc., the number-one manufacturer of man-sized tissue products in the U.S.A.

DON'T DO DAINTY!

Rough Tissues for Tough Men *

Tissues impregnated with finely-ground glass particles for that reassuringly rugged, manly wipe.

* Now with our "They'll Make Your Nose Bleed" Guarantee – or your money back!

Also available as toilet tissue.

Sneezy-Snout Inc. is a member of the Foundation for the Encouragement of Men's Art, Literature and Education (F.E.M.A.L.E.) and is proud to be associated with *Call Me Randy: The Cowboy Tales of Randall J. Jackson*

CALL ME RANDY

The Cowboy Tales of Randall J. Jackson

Contents

Prologue	7
Editor's Introduction	11
Randall Jackson's Introduction	13
Daisy	15
The Naked Beach	19
Gunfight at Skull Creek	23
Tucson Threesome	33
Wedding Vows	43
Bounty Hunter I: The Legend of Annie James	47
Bounty Hunter II: The Rough Justice of Arnold Pecker	57
Lady Jane	63
The Fountain	69
The Scarecrow Maker	75
Angels of Matrimony	83
The Taming of Randy	93
The Wrath of Skull Creek	99
Epilogue	113
Bonus Feature: An Editor's Tale	117
Acknowledgements	123

Prologue

They come to me in my dreams, night after night…

A cloud of red canyon dust grows on the horizon, like the first warning wisps of a tornado. It hurtles towards me from the distant West, swelling like an angry swarm.

The sound at first is faint; light drumming, nothing more. But it grows, a pulse that beats in my head like a hammering heartbeat. The thunderous hooves of heavy beasts kick dirt high into the sky, enveloping five riders.

A cruel sun beats fiercely down, baking skin that glistens with sweat and grime from countless days spent pounding desert trails. Blistering heat and wind-driven sands have cracked open lips and hardened spirits.

In the centre of the small posse, a sole woman rides with the same driven purpose as the rough men that surround her. A voice whispers *Annie James* in my head. Strangely, instinctively, I know that she is the great, great, great-granddaughter of the notorious train robber and killer, Jesse James. She is a bounty hunter. Her breasts jiggle crazily as the white mare gallops beneath her.

There are two men flanking Annie - Frank and Jesse. They glance sideways at the arousing bounce of female flesh and grin across at each other, faces flecked with stubble and streaked with dirt.

The front rider turns his head at intervals, also noting the tempting display. He is amused by the hypnotic effect it has on the closest of his male friends. He is a little older than his companions, and is happy in the knowledge that it is he who will rest his head on the pillow of Annie's breasts at the end of their arduous journey, so long as they are not too bruised and sensitive. But he will try to lay his head there regardless.

At the rear of the posse is Jed, the youngest rider by a few years. His face is weathered but handsome. His blue eyes show softness as they stare past

Annie to admire the leading man's butt, which is gently smacked by the torn and time-worn leather of saddle with every stride of the black stallion beneath. Jed would like to smack it too, only a bit harder. He hopes to lay his head on its reassuring pertness as he sleeps after the toils of a punishing day. It's pretty unlikely but, knowing Jed, he will try his luck anyway, unwilling to give up on his dream.

Frank stops staring at Annie's cleavage to deeply pick his nose. He frowns in concentration and wipes nuggets as precious as gold on his horse's mane. The horse snorts with indignation.

The relentless stampede brings the billowing dust cloud ever closer. The driving force of a sandstorm kicks up around the riders, stinging ears and cheeks as they chase balls of tumbleweed that roll across the plains in their path. The skeletal bales of brush fracture and break like fragile bird-bones, spreading seeds. But so singled-minded are the cowboys, united in their mission, that all obstacles serve to increase their resolve and spur them on.

They are five. They are magnificent.

I shall call them *The Splendid Five*.

As if in protest at my pronouncement, reins are tugged, while dust in the air blurs my vision. I'm enveloped in fine sand that settles, as five horses emerge from the dissipating cloud, slowing from a gallop to a canter. They draw to a halt in front of me, fully emerging from the orange-red haze that drops powder on the lapels of my nightshirt. I brush it off, irritated, but too afraid to let it show.

I only had the nightshirt laundered yesterday.

The riders tower above me on horseback. I feel myself tensing. They glance around, and then turn to face me as one. I release a small amount of nervous wind. And something else slips through.

"What… what do you want from me…?" I squeak hesitantly, apprehension mounting. "Whatever it is, you can have it… my Dolly Parton CDs… my Clint Eastwood Blu-rays… just take them…"

The leading man dismounts while the others slowly begin to circle me, their horses' hooves clicking. I am about to plead… no, to *beg* for my life, but the approaching cowboy's intensity silences me. His features are craggy, creases deep around the eyes. His hands rest on holstered weapons. I am petrified. He draws up close and I smell whiskey on his breath. Three words tumble from his lips, gruff, hard. But his eyes sparkle with mischief. I can tell he has lived long, and fought and played hard. A womaniser, for sure.

Notorious. He repeats the three words in a slow drawl. The three words all women long to hear…

"Call me Randy."

He reaches into his back pocket as if to retrieve something, and then stretches a gnarled hand towards me, proffering a fistful of dollars. His other hand eases and lifts a gun in its holster, as if daring me to decline. I'm not going to argue. I take the crumpled bundle as if making a pact with the devil, and squeeze my eyes tightly shut in trepidation. When I open them, the strange posse has disappeared.

I awaken in the swivel chair in front of my computer screen and keyboard. I sigh with relief… it was just a bad dream…

But there is a stack of worn dollar bills by the mouse mat. A draught must have caught the untidy pile as, on my lap, there are a few dollars more.

The notes are ancient and bigger than modern currency. I look down at the bald eagle perched on an American flag. Beneath it are two smaller images of Abraham Lincoln and Ulysses S. Grant. I'm certain the bills are no longer in circulation. Who knows, they may be worth more than their face value on eBay? Besides, it is a fee of sorts. And I know what is expected…

I glance at the clock on the wall as a cuckoo flies out of the hatch, announcing four o'clock in the morning. I decide to head up to bed but, like every other night this month, I hear Randy's voice, which continues its incessant drawl inside my brain. His voice torments me night and day, insistent in its demands and urgency. I can't ignore it if I ever hope to break free from this madness. I must complete the task.

I hear Randy chuckle as my hands reach out and start tapping the keys.

He has stories to tell…

I pause, brushing fine sand particles from my shoulders. There is something on my collar too. It is moist and repugnant. *Frank!* I understand for a moment how Frank's horse must feel. Then my fingers begin their frenzied dance as I sink into a trance-like state, obediently stabbing out the words whispered in my ear…

…someone shouts… a scream echoes off deep canyon walls… frightened horses squeal… bullets ricochet… and something evil cackles…

Something spawned in hell. There is death on the horizon.

I shudder.

The forces of good and evil are about to collide in a desert furnace.
Men will fall.
Legends will rise...

...An epic Western adventure begins...

Editor's Introduction

To enjoy Randall J. Jackson's poetry and performance is to admit that there still remains a dark, yet vibrantly alive place inside you. In order to fully appreciate his work, it is essential to find your own inner cowboy voice. Try practising the following line, as a slow drawl, to cultivate your authentic Wild West accent, before undertaking this fascinating, yet disturbing journey:

English:

I'd really quite like you to leave, if you don't mind.

Arizonian pronunciation (U.S. of A.):

If ya don't git your goddamn hide outta here, I'll fill it fulla bullet holes!

Alternatively, why not try:

English:

I certainly didn't intend to make you feel in any way uptight or offended.

Arizonian pronunciation (U.S. of A.):

Uh shaw didn't mean to git you orl ur-pi-tee and O-fin-did.

In reality, having studied Jackson's material in depth for several years, I believe he intended his work to be challenging and, at times, to cause deliberate offence. Paradoxically, he also seems an extraordinarily open-minded and tolerant man, embracing human difference, naturism, and as many women as he can.

I have only made small alterations to Jackson's work where overwhelming violations of good taste have occurred but, broadly speaking, his poems are presented here as they were originally written during the earlier decades of the 1900s. Jackson's subsequent career performing his poetry only began in the middle of the 1960s.

Jackson's comments, which follow in his separate introduction as well as in his preamble to a number of the poems, are Jackson's own original words taken directly from recordings made at the various venues (mainly across the U.S.A.) where he recited his poetry.

Jackson gives what many believe is the most authentic depiction of the lawless Wild West, which, despite the advances of the early twentieth century, persevered in many remote, time-frozen pockets of the western states, and particularly in the "desert southwest", well into the 1930s.

I am pleased to say that Jackson, born in 1899, is still alive and well today, although he no longer makes personal appearances. This selection has been produced with Jackson's somewhat grudging permission as, when I first approached him with the idea a year ago, he was short of cash to meet the ongoing care needs of his frail, elderly wife, Billie-Jo.

Many people who have studied Jackson's material have asked: Do Jackson's poems and monologues illuminate the underlying fragility of human relationships yet, at the same time, reveal useful insights and guiding wisdom to assist people in their noble journeys from infancy to maturity, by altering their perceptions and enabling them to reach a more compassionate and spiritual approach to their lives and relationships? After my own extensive exploration of his work, I can reveal the answer: No. They do not.

Stuart L. Groom, London, England, March 2011

Randall Jackson's Introduction

From a live show at the Stardust casino, Las Vegas, Nevada, during Jackson's second series of performances, the "Alimony" comeback tour, 14 April 1969.

Howdy fellas. Ladies. I come from a rugged ol' town called Carter's Bluff in Arizona – you mighta heard of it? It's close to the border with Utah, and I'm known there as *The Cowboy Poet*, Randall J. Jackson. But, hell – you can call me Randy. Especially the ladies!

I feel mighty proud to be sharin' some of my poems with you tonight. I think they capture the beauty and danger of the Wild West in all its savage and unpredictable glory. You'll hopefully agree, as I do, that cowboy poetry is the finest poetry – not just in the Wild West – but in the whole damn world.

Before we get started, there's somethin' you need to know about me, and that's the fact that I've been married eighteen times, especially as my wives are the inspiration behind a lot of the poetry I've written. Now, I know what you're thinkin'. You're askin' yourselves, "How come someone as goddamn handsome as ol' Randy here has only had eighteen wives?" Well, I sure as hell don't blame you for wonderin' that as I find it mighty vexatious myself. But I always recognise that it's a sign of an intelligent audience that it crossed your minds straight away.

Anyhow, I've learned a heck of a lot from the ladies in my life, especially my wives. And some of those things have changed me as a man. Take, for instance, my first wife, Susannah. She taught me the value of personal hygiene. By divorcin' me!

I still think that was kind of a liberty on her part, especially when you consider that she was known to most folk by the nickname of "Windy Sue".

You'd know exactly why they called her that if you'd ever had to share the back of a stagecoach with her.

I remember one time – a very sad occasion. A close friend of mine had passed away real young. His name was Jake and we held a little ceremony for him at the chapel on the hill, soon after he died. Now Jake's daughter – pretty little thing – she lit a candle for her daddy. And at that exact same moment the entire congregation lost their eyebrows and their hair. Well I had a pretty good idea about the source of the gas escape that caused the incident. Let's just say that my Susannah – she didn't need to wax her lady-parts for a very long time after that.

Anyhow, I'm kinda gettin' ahead of myself here and squawkin' on like a rooster catchin' his first glimpse o' the mornin' sun. So I'll get right on with my first poem. This one's about another of my wives, Daisy. It's called "Daisy". And so was she.

Daisy

***A woman known to some folk as
"Detachable Dee"***

My Daisy was a beauty with a proud look in her eye;
she only had the one, which sometimes suffered from a stye.
But her legs were smooth and shapely, as a short skirt would reveal,
though I preferred, if truth be told, the leg that wasn't real.
The only problem, strokin' her from ankle up to thigh,
was sometimes I'd get splinters diggin' deep, and tough to ply.

Now, even in the Wild West, medicine was quite advanced,
so I took her to a surgeon to be surgically enhanced.
Her breasts, once little fried eggs, grew beyond a double D.
I'd sneak up and release the clasp to set those puppies free.
Her bra was made from parachutes to keep those beasts in check
and all heads turned when Daisy passed, and some yelled, "Hootin' heck!"

We laughed a lot. Such precious times of fun and liberty.
I'd walk with Daisy's arm in mine, as proud as I could be.
She'd seem a bit distracted, but I loved her – didn't mind,
until I noticed that I'd left the rest of her behind.
But Daisy seemed to be a goddess, pure and heaven sent,
and every inch a woman – well, at least 50 per cent.

Now, way out West the sun beats down so fierce a man could fry,
so Daisy smeared protective lotion on my back and sides -
a normal brand, not fancy stuff that leaves an orange tarnish.
And in return I'd sand her down, then reapply her varnish.
The way she'd touch my skin with hands so soft could get me frisky.
And she enjoyed my bristly brush on her, after a whiskey.

We'd head off to a nudist camp we loved, from time to time,
way up in the mountains with some cowboys of like mind.
The nights up there got pretty cold. We'd huddle 'round a fire,
all pink and drunk and naked, and arousin' some desire.
Now cowboys can be mighty rough and ladies get quite scared,
but Daisy was detachable and easy to be shared.

I think she liked those times the most, when cowboys took her back
to separate tents at the same time, to frolic in the sack.
But sadly Daisy's life was short, and ended brightly lit.
A fireside spark caught Daisy's leg, while she was wearin' it.
I missed her bad at first and, in my dreams, cried out her name.
I'd wake to find her in my bed - a ghostly ball of flame.

I ain't no coward; all the same, I found it kinda creepy.
She'd lie upon my latest wife who'd scream and get quite weepy.
I'd have to reassure her, the only way a man knows how,
but she'd say I'm insensitive as sweat dripped off my brow.
So I employed an exorcist, which worked, we both presume.
But why can I smell varnish sometimes, waftin' 'round the room?

Arm in arm with detachable Daisy

The Naked Beach

From a live performance at the Silver Spur casino, Reno ("the biggest little city in the world"), Nevada, during Jackson's "An Itch in My Chaps" tour, 25 August 1977.

I don't want you fine fellas and ladies gettin' the impression that tragedy and misfortune only befall the women in my life, 'cause it just ain't true.

My next poem is gonna emphasise the pain of bein' a man in the Wild West, somethin' most ladies don't give a second thought to. But I think this will bring a tear to everyone's eyes. It certainly did to mine.

Before I carry on, I notice some of you fellas looking at me kinda strange. I'm wonderin' if you've noticed that these chaps I'm wearin' are, in fact, ladies' chaps. Well I don't want you thinkin' I didn't know that. I just prefer the look and feel of ladies' chaps, as they fit snugger than men's. In fact, sometimes, back in the privacy of my own ranch, these are the only things I wear! Now ain't that a pretty picture for all of you ladies here tonight! I'm guessin' that even a few of you fellas are findin' it pleasin' in a way that's makin' you question yourselves. But don't let it worry you none. It ain't your fault that I'm such a goddamn temptation on account of my good looks and mighty fine legs. And as you can see, my age ain't diminished that – not even a bit!

But I've been a naturist right back since my teenage years, as you'll probably have guessed from my reference to a nudist camp in the last poem. And by a stroke o' luck, most of my wives have shared my keen interest in naturism and found it just as liberatin' as I do.

As you know, we have some fine beaches in the West. Not just on the Pacific coastline, but also at some of our natural and man made lakes, such as Lake Mead, Lake Powell, and – if you don't mind travellin' a bit further – even Lake Tahoe where the sparklin' emerald waters are prettier than the finest lady's eyes that you ever gazed into with a sense of love in your heart and lust in your pants. I'm sure most of you have been to Lake Tahoe, but back in the ol' days, if you knew where to go, there was also a section of its shores given over to nudist bathin'. Unofficially and totally illegally of course.

However, there were always some hidden perils to naturism in the Wild West, and that's what my next poem is all about. It's called "The Naked Beach". You'll see I've snuck in a modern reference, which I like to do from time to time, just so you fellas and ladies don't think I'm totally divorced from the modern world. Anyhow, I sure hope you like it.

The Naked Beach

A tale known to some folk as
"The Perils of Wild West Naturism"

I've always been a naturist, so bodies plump or slender
no longer shock or scandalise in any shape or gender.
I think the sight of humans bare is natural as can be.
Most folks glance to satisfy their curiosity
then shrug as if to say "So what? It ain't a mighty fuss"
and get on with their bathin' till they take the homeward bus.

My second wife, called Trudy, searched for danger in the sun.
We'd lay our towels out and, between 'em, place a loaded gun.
Provokin' for attention was the thing that got her thrilled.
She was the kind o' lady who could get her husband killed.
She'd left a string of men in early graves on Tombstone Hill,
includin' Lightnin' Larry, Lucky Lance and Winnin' Will.

One time, we'd barely shed our clothes and laid out on the beach;
she started flickin' pebbles at two guys in easy reach.
The biggest one came over, askin' me, "What's goin' on?"
I bluffed, "It's just a greetin' that's quite friendly where we're from."
But Trudy told him straight, to take a hike and move away
if little pranks and playfulness were ruinin' his day.

He must have seen I'd placed my hand beside my gun, in case
he tried to start a fight and bruise ol' Randy's pretty face.
He scowled at her and glared at me, retreatin' with a huff.
I'd have to stay alert, as he was naked, mean and buff.
But I was tired and drifted off. Bad dreams ran through my head
of bein' chased by men who wore no clothes and wished me dead.

Then Trudy's voice awoke me and I sensed her slight alarm.
I reached out for my weapon but she quickly blocked my arm.
She said, "Keep still, a giant wasp has landed on your johnson".
I hate those critters; felt my fear arisin' somethin' awesome.
Her worry turned to giggles. She put down her ice-cream cornet.
I was less amused – I knew that bastard was a hornet.

She got it in her head to strike before the beast could sting
and whacked it with her novel – somethin' fat by Stephen King.
Well, had it been a slimmer tome it might have hurt less bad.
The hornet stung me anyhow – I shrieked like I was mad.
I leapt around the beach, attractin' every pair of eyes,
which widened as my balls flared up – ten times their normal size!

The guys that she'd tormented earlier laughed until they cried.
You'd think they'd show some sympathy; instead they split their sides.
I ran into the lake to hide my balls from those ashore,
but they floated on the surface like two Portuguese Men-Of-War.
My shame and anger fought as, through my veins, the venom coursed.
Before the swellin' settled, me and Trudy were divorced.

"I reckon that's the only reason I'm still alive today" – **R.J. Jackson**

Gunfight at Skull Creek

From a live performance at Caesar's Palace casino, Las Vegas, Nevada, during Jackson's "More Than One Way to Skin a Coyote" tour, 12 May 1995.

There's a time in my life I don't often talk about, way back when I was barely twenty and before I'd even been married for the first time. I was more of a wanderer back then, with barely a dime to my name and often relyin' on the charity of close friends like Jake, Frank and Jesse and the company of generous women, if you take my meanin'. One time on my travels I passed through the notorious town of Skull Creek.

An interestin' fact about Skull Creek is that it ain't even near a source of runnin' water, and all the water they got back then had to be piped in. However, that was just down to global warmin'. Back in the early 1800s it was sittin' on a river that's long since evaporated in the blisterin' desert heat.

Skull Creek takes its name from a massacre of the earliest settlers by the Native Americans who believed it was their rightful territory, before they were finally forced onto the reservations and domesticated with the help of cheap liquor and the threat of a bullet to the brain. But legend has it that the Indians butchered the settlers and left the river runnin' red for several days. The scalped and decapitated heads of the settlers clung to the roots of trees and cacti on the banks of the river, bobbin' with sightless eyes, and starin' like a warnin' to all passers by.

It's said that the town had always had bad karma, and everyone that lived there or passed through it were prone to be affected by the restless spirits of the Indian elders who were still angry at the takin' of their lands. Personally, I reckon it was more to do with the lead in the ol' water pipes, which were the last to be replaced, and affected the brains of the townsfolk.

When I arrived at Skull Creek all those years ago, I didn't give a damn about its reputation as a snake pit of villains that was best avoided. I was full of youthful notions and arrogant pride, and I reckoned I could cope with anything life could throw at me. I was even excited at the prospect of enterin' the meanest and wildest town in the West, and discoverin' what all the fuss was about. Didn't take me long to realise I'd made an awful mistake.

This is the tale of my visit there. I've changed only one line of the poem since I wrote it, to update it for a modern audience. I do that from time to time, as poetic licence allows. So there's a reference to a film from 1972, but all the events actually took place in 1919. And those events have haunted me one way or another ever since.

Pram-rage at Skull Creek

Gunfight at Skull Creek

A town known to some folk as
"The Roughest, Toughest Town in the West"

I knew I'd made a bad mistake the day I stopped to rest
in Skull Creek, Arizona, meanest town in all the West.
Everywhere I wandered, fists were flyin', guns were drawn
and every misbehavin' kid was staked out on the lawn.

You didn't want to take the risk of gettin' folk upset.
They'd shoot you just for winnin' any fair and honest bet.
I stopped at a saloon to take a bourbon for my fear
but couldn't reach the bar for rowdy women swiggin' beer.

Outside, they'd left their prams and buggies tethered to a rail,
containin' babies dressed in pink despite them bein' male.
And every babe was wavin' loaded guns like playground toys
and glarin' at the ribbons on the other pigtailed boys.

I ducked as one boy fired, and felt the round go through my hat.
The little villain looked so pleased, he giggled as he shat.
The row of infants kicked their legs and bit their teddies' ears,
while all the drunken mothers cussed inside and supped their beers.

I stopped by the latrine as I was bustin' for a pee
and felt confused that women stood at either side of me.
I trembled, johnson in my hand, but dared to sneak a peak,
afraid to glance but curious how those ladies took a leak.

Sometimes I still have flashbacks and I wish I hadn't looked.
I understood why some men stayed at home and cleaned 'n' cooked.
I shook so hard to finish fast, a few drops splashed my face,
then fled to play some poker, where my hand held every ace.

I won a prize – to stay an extra night at Nancy's Inn!
Well ain't that just the kind o' thing that no man wants to win!
I sloped off to a hardware store to buy the biggest bolt
to make my hotel room secure while sleepin' with my Colt.

All night long the yellin' flared and countless bullets fired.
I barely slept a wink and hugged my pillow, wakin' tired.
I breakfasted with coffee, tryin' to get myself awake;
then heard a sound to curdle blood. My hands began to shake.

I noticed, through a window, ladies gathered in the square,
encirclin' some outsider on his knees, who they'd stripped bare.
Now I recalled "Deliverance" when they made the piggy squeal.
Each lady used a cattle prod. I brought up half my meal.

I took a shower, the water cold, but didn't make a fuss;
a sign at the reception said that guests who whinged or cussed
would spend an hour in the stocks, then find themselves well hung.
I saw the joke, but couldn't laugh - I'd seen their take on fun.

To be a bad man in Skull Creek, you sure had competition,
but with balls the size of war bags and some heavy ammunition
you could make your mark in bullet holes on every swingin' door
and leave a thick deposit on the finest Skull Creek whore.

I saddled Stan, my horse, at speed, intendin' to depart,
but bumped into a man who'd transformed evil to an art.
He said, "Hey cowboy, dance for me!" and blasted at my feet.
Though I'm no good at dainty moves, I stepped out pretty neat.

But he got bored and aimed his barrel squarely at my head.
Who'd have thought I'd learn to dance the day I'd wind up dead?
I spun and pranced and shimmied, tryin' to please that evil dude,
as circlin' buzzards licked their beaks, regardin' me as food.

The bastard chuckled, sayin', "Quit that jig, your dancin's fine.
I'll save my bullet; just leave town before I change my mind."
I told him, "I'm a poet, and I'll write about this place."
He laughed, insistin', "Poets are all queer and a disgrace!"

Well, I felt my dander risin' for all poets he'd insulted.
My gun leapt to my hand and fired. Blood sprayed and wounds erupted.
He'd never harm another man. I left that town with pride,
while cowboys backed away in fear, gun smokin' at my side.

I didn't even fret about the forces of the law,
as someone shot the sheriff dead about a week before.
I galloped out o' town onto the windswept desert plains,
until I found a waterhole and tugged my horse's reins.

I gazed into the water, where I noticed, on inspection,
apart from guns, I seemed to wear no clothes in my reflection.
But I was wearin' make-up, and a fresh tattoo spelled "granny".
I'd also got a shard of tooth embedded in my fanny.

I looked at Stan, dismayed. He twitched his ears and huffed aloud.
I'd swear he was embarrassed, shufflin' dust into a cloud.
I'd lost my hat and memory too – I'd stayed an extra night.
I must have jiggled as I danced and looked a sorry sight.

But worst of all were dreams that left me vexed and soaked in sweat,
as strands of recollection fought my yearnin' to forget.
I sure was glad I'd left that place, though some folk were impressed
that Skull Creek legend named me "Finest Dancer in the West".

"I'm tellin' ya, Stanley, I can't remember!"

Tucson Threesome

From a live performance at Cliffs Pavilion, Southend-on-Sea, Essex, England, during Jackson's "Twilight Remembrance" tour, 15 March 2007.

Howdy fellas. Ladies. This is only my second tour in the U.K. and, at my age, I reckon it's time I retired from life on the road – especially now my Billie-Jo needs the extra care and support back home.

Since arrivin' in your fine country, I've been hearin' a lot about the pleasin' reputation of you Essex gals. You can call me Randy, by the way. Now I'm a generous ol' cowboy so, as a special treat, my dressin' room will be open for business after the show. Please form an orderly queue outside while waitin' your turn, and try not to overexcite yourselves. I'd hate for you to peak too soon and miss some genuine Wild West action, though I can understand how it could happen on account of my craggy good looks. Hell, I gaze at myself naked in the mirror every mornin' and find I overexcite myself too! Though it takes a little longer these days.

This tour – bein' the last – takes a rose-tinted look at the best o' times from my youth and the people that made a tough life in a hostile world worth endurin' – a time when friendship was more valuable than all the gold in the Rocky Mountains. I'm gonna begin by turnin' the clock back to the early 1920s to share a tale of friendship as powerful as the parable of the Good Samaritan.

While I was married to my first wife, Susannah, I lost my close friend Jake to a rattlesnake bite in Bryce Canyon. He might have survived the rattler if he hadn't yanked his pants down to suck out the venom and sat his bare butt on the nearest rock. It was durin' the height of the matin' season for scorpions, and he failed to spot a pair of 'em makin' out on his chosen seat. The extra dose of poison was too much for his heart to take. I doubt the scorpions appreciated their final moments either, as Jake's backside blotted out the sun and headed towards them like some weird kind of asteroid covered in ginger hair.

You may not know this, but rattlesnake venom slowly and painfully dissolves tissue and twists bone. Poor ol' Jake was a bloated and misshapen mess by the time he was found, with a squashed scorpion stuck to each buttock. They had to bury him in the strangest shaped coffin I've ever seen just to accommodate all his weird angles and swollen flesh. There was no dignity in his death, that's for sure.

The family had Jake's body on view at the chapel with the casket open for a while, but everyone – includin' his family – kept yakkin' up at the sight of him. It didn't seem fair to leave Jake swimmin' in vomit, so the coffin-maker was summoned to nail the lid down. That fella won a design award for his tailor-made coffin, makin' him mighty proud. It also transformed his firm into the top undertakin' business in Arizona. As you can imagine, with all the lawless behaviour out West there was a fortune to be made in the undertakin' business – though competition was stiff. No… That wasn't meant to be a joke… I'd appreciate it if you'd quit your laughin'…

Thank you.

Anyhow, I counted myself lucky I still had my close buddies, Frank and Jesse, but we missed Jake real bad. If a man's to stay alive in the Wild West, he needs as many good friends as he can get.

I remember bein' at the graveside with Frank, Jesse and all the relatives when Jake was finally laid to rest. I thought I saw the coffin-maker slip a bundle of dollars to Jake's widow while the preacher was spoutin' his nonsense. Then the coffin-maker winked at the preacher who immediately asked the gathered crowd to close their eyes in prayer. Now I ain't one for prayer, so I kept my peepers wide open, wonderin' what the heck was goin' on.

While everyone was contemplatin' the preacher's words, two pallbearers standin' by the coffin knelt and yanked the nails out of the coffin lid and removed it. I caught a glimpse of my ol' friend and it broke my heart to see him messed up so bad. The pallbearers lifted the coffin over the grave and tipped Jake's body out into the burial pit, then rushed the designer-casket back to the horse-drawn hearse, where the coffin-maker handed them a standard coffin lid. They sprinted back to the graveside with the lid and dropped it on top of Jake. Then the preacher winked at the grave-digger who started shovellin' earth into the pit. By the time the preacher said "Amen" – at the end of the longest prayer I've ever heard – they'd pretty much covered up what they'd done.

I found out that the coffin-maker couldn't bear to have his prize-winnin' creation covered up with dirt. He sold the casket for a stack o' dollars to the first ever Museum of Modern Art in New York, though us cowboys didn't know what "modern art" meant at the time. I'm not sure many people know what it means today.

I paid the coffin-maker a visit as soon as I could, with Frank and Jesse, to teach him some respect. He wouldn't have been able to hammer a nail into a jellyfish for a long time afterwards. And as the cryin' coffin-maker watched us leave that day, we all made a point of winkin' at him – real slow.

All the same, it barely scratched the surface of our grief, so we were mighty pleased when another fella came into our lives in an unexpected way, soon after Jake died. And that's the story I want to tell you right now, from 1922. But despite this good news, fate had somethin' else in store for us. I regret to inform you that we weren't all destined for long and happy lives. When the storm finally hit, I couldn't even bring myself to grieve, as I felt partly responsible. But don't let that spoil your enjoyment of this earlier tale...

Tucson Threesome

***A tale known to some folk as
"The Two Cowboy Samaritans"***

My closest pals were Frank and Jesse, from my teenage years;
as loyal as dogs, though some said little happened 'tween their ears.
What Frank and Jesse lacked in smarts they made good with their hands,
which wandered over ladies all across the Western lands,
but also skilled at carpentry, built ranches, bars and schools.
They toiled and sweltered in the desert heat with woodwork tools.
They hoped to wed, but women found the lifestyle too extreme,
so when the boys hit Tucson for supplies they'd let off steam.

I guess you'd say that Frank was handsome; dark with deep blue eyes,
while Jesse was tattooed and fit, with sculpted arms and thighs.
Though Jesse was the dimmest of the pair, Frank could astound;
sometimes he'd mount his saddle and end up the wrong way 'round.
The ladies at the Tucson brothels fought for Frank and Jess,
each claiming rights to have them first, and desperate to impress.
So Frank and Jesse tried to please as many as they could
despite the fact they'd only stopped the night to get some wood.

Those boys were so darned popular, while other men got barred,
the finest whorehouse gave them both a brothel loyalty card.
For every nine paid visits they would get the tenth for free
and twenty per cent discount at the bar on brands of tea.
I don't think that impressed them much. When offered Lady Grey
they thought a high-class whore – not *tea* that sucks – would come their way.
One time, in Tucson, both tried out a new saloon, The Stud,
where guys were awful friendly and one bought them each a Bud.

When Jess was young, a girl called Sammie broke his cowboy heart,
but then along came Billie-May. Jess thought they'd never part
until an out-of-towner won her over with his charms.
All Jesse had to show for love were tattoos on his arms.
Now, at The Stud, with sleeves rolled up, the eyes of every man
admired his bold tattoos, as one spelled "BILL", the other "SAM".
It took a while, but Frank twigged first; some guy pinched his behind.
Turned out The Stud was first saloon to open of its kind.

Frank took a hold of Jesse; steered him straight towards the door
and said to Jess, "Forget the beer, let's get ourselves a whore".
"But Frank," said Jess, "We can't walk out. We owe that man a drink."
But Frank exclaimed, "Just leave! He's after more than beer, I think."
The brothel soon eased Frank's disquiet, but Jess remained confused,
so Frank drew Jess a detailed sketch, which left him quite bemused.
"I just don't see the problem, Frank. Sometimes I like it better.
In fact I've done the same myself tonight with young Loretta."

They headed for their hotel past The Stud and, lyin' hurt,
a man was being kicked by several cowboys in the dirt.
The friends despised an unfair fight and, like avenging Gods,
they waded in with boot and fist to even up the odds.
The fella being beaten was the guy who'd bought them beer,
and neither thought that he should suffer just for bein' queer.
The fightin' bullies soon were moanin', curled up on the ground;
six of them to Frank and Jesse, lyin' all around.

One looked up, about to stand, intent on causin' harm,
but Jesse clenched a fist and muscles rippled on his arm.
The cowboy stared in horror, seein' words spelt "SAM" and "BILL".
He'd never met a queer before that looked like he would kill.
The foes retreated. Frank and Jesse barely had a bruise,
though Frank advised his friend to quickly cover his tattoos.
They dragged the victim to his feet, who groaned and seemed concussed,
and Jess said, "He's a mess – we'd better take him back with us."

They stripped the young man's bloody, tattered shirt and cleaned him up,
and bathed the swollen, purple eyes that marred the wounded pup.
They pushed their beds together, givin' space enough for three
and laid the man between 'em, who was squintin' hard to see.
He mumbled, "Is this heaven, boys? I can't believe my luck.
I hate to disappoint you, though. I'm in no state to… Fuck,
I usually introduce myself before I share a bed.
I ain't no hustler, I'm a wrangler mostly known as Jed!"

With that, he passed out, snorin' loud enough to wake the town,
but woke up first and quickly slid beneath the eiderdown.
Both Frank and Jesse thought they dreamed of fun with girlfriends past.
You've never seen two macho men leap out of bed so fast!
The source of their false notions grinned and said, "Good mornin' guys.
Just checkin' I've no fingers broke, by opening button-flies!"
It seemed that Jed made up with cheek for all he lacked in sense,
so Frank laid down some rules, while Jesse taught him self-defence.

Jed came to live in Carter's Bluff and soon became a friend.
I sure felt blessed to have three pals on whom I could depend.
Jed helped his two Samaritans with building work some days,
and then became my wranglin' partner, herdin' up the strays.
We worked and played and all seemed well. And Jess met Daniella.
He loved her, though it didn't last. She found another fella.
The final straw was Jesse bein' such a stupid man,
he got himself a huge tattoo proclaimin' love for "DAN".

Sweetly dreamin' of girlfriends past

Wedding Vows

From a live performance at the Moonshine Lodge, Emerald Bay, Lake Tahoe, during Jackson's "Call Me Randy" tour, 13 September 1987.

I'm sure I've mentioned to you fine people before that I've been married eighteen times. Often people come up to me and ask, "Hey, Randy, what's the secret of a successful marriage?" Well, if I had any sense I oughtta say to them, "I'll let you know as soon as I've had one". But what I tend to say, based on my considerable experience, is, "Keep 'em short". By which I mean the marriages, not the women. Although my fourth wife, Pixie, was the shortest woman I've ever met. At the same time – she was exactly the right height for one thing. I was very happy in that marriage. Shame it was all over so quick. The marriage, I mean. Though I recall her sayin' the same thing quite often while we were together.

Anyhow, I'm digressin' again. The truth - and everybody really knows this – is that the secret to a good marriage is keepin' the romance alive. And ever since my sixth marriage, to Daisy, I've been startin' as I mean to go on, by writin' my own weddin' vows, which I thought I'd share with you here today.

When I recite these vows, I find that all the ladies in the congregation get mighty weepy on account of the beautiful poetry that exposes the raw cowboy heart. So I'm kinda warnin' you that if you're in an open or emotionally vulnerable space, you might wanna have yourself a handkerchief ready.

In fact, sometimes when I've shared these vows, even the toughest ol' cowboys come up to me afterwards, eyes all puffy and red from cryin'. And they'll say somethin' like, "Hey Randy, those are just about the prettiest words I ever did hear. Now I'm marryin' my fiancé next summer and I'd be mighty obliged if you'd let me use those vows at our weddin'". Well, I always say, "Sure fella, it'd be my privilege." The way I figure it, it's just another way of spreadin' a bit of love into the world. And that's pretty much what my whole life's been about

So, if any of you good folk are about to get married, or even plannin' to reaffirm your weddin' vows, I'd be honoured and happy for you to use mine, which I sometimes call "Randy's Recipe for Romancin'".

I should mention that I've taken the poetic liberty of usin' a word the Brits use for a "saloon" or "bar". It's the word "pub", which is short for a "public house" and it don't mean a brothel. So here we go with the most beautiful weddin' vows – not just in the Wild West – but in the whole damn world.

Wedding Vows

*The solemn promises known to some folk as
"Randy's Recipe for Romancin' "*

I promise to be faithful, darlin' – as often as I can.
I'll give up rustlin' cattle. I won't sleep with any man,
except my wranglin' partner, Jed, when drunk from guzzlin' beers;
but that don't count, my angel – we've been doin' it for years.

And when you've cooked my supper, as sleep binds you in its threads,
just leave the washin' up, my love; don't worry your sweet head.
So slumber softly in my arms until the new day's dawnin' –
you can wash the dishes when you've cooked my breakfast in the mornin'.

To stress my firm commitment, pumpkin, till we're old and grey,
I promise to improve my hygiene, washin' every day
at least my face and hands, and once a week my 'pits and feet.
And every month I'll rinse my johnson, just to keep you sweet.

I'll never pester you for sex, unless my sap is risin',
and lately that's just twice a day, which I find quite surprisin'.
I think I'll see a doctor; that won't leave the gals impressed.
For cowboys, only twice a day is vergin' on disinterest.

I won't expect you to obey or always think I'm right.
Refrain from disagreein' though – I'll keep you warm at night;
especially in the winter, when I come back from the pub.
I'll breathe upon your pretty face and give your breasts a rub.

And when we've finished kissin', an' makin' love without a rush,
I'll clip my dirty fingernails and give my teeth a brush.
I'll turn my back on brothel doors – every time I leave one!
But even when I'm with a whore I'll think of you, my sweet one.

All these vows I'll keep to show my deepest love for you.
Can't promise it's forever, but I hope a while will do.
So take this ring and be my wife. Luck found you – you're a winner.
Now saddle up, come to my ranch, and swiftly make my dinner.

"I don't think you'll find a more romantic set of weddin' vows in any place on Earth. They've come straight from the cowboy's heart" – **Randall J. Jackson**

Bounty Hunter I:
The Legend of Annie James

From a live performance at The Horseshoe Club casino, Reno, Nevada, during Jackson's "A Horse Called Stan" tour, 8 May 1994.

Howdy fellas. Ladies. I was last in Reno back in 1977 when I first brought my poetry recital show, "An Itch in My Chaps", to the Silver Spur. Back then, as I'm sure you know, it was next-door to the original Horseshoe Club but has now been merged to become a part of it. I was still gettin' accustomed to performin' the material that I'd been writin' for most of my life, and was very grateful at the time for an appreciative audience. I guess I didn't have as much confidence in my writin' as I have today, and wasn't sure how long my run o' success would last and whether folks would stay interested in the poetic ramblings of an old man.

If you wish to show your gratitude tonight, you can do so by buyin' me a beer between poems. You won't understand a word I'm sayin' by the end of the evenin' but I'll still be lookin' mighty handsome all the same. I ain't bad for ninety-somethin' and even my johnson's in perfect workin' order. I'm guessin' - by the looks on your faces - that you really didn't want to know that.

Of all the material I've written, the stuff that folks seem to like the best is about the legendary bounty hunter, Annie James – who also happened to be my wife at one time. Strangely, she was also the only woman who ever liked my horse, Stanley. I guess Stan was more of a man's horse and, after all, in the Wild West, a horse is a man's best friend. You'll probably be hearin' more about Stan later, dependin' on how much I've had to drink by then.

Annie was the bravest woman in the West and most folk know of her reputation even today. She was a damn good bounty hunter and the most successful of all time, even against the fellas.

Annie was the great, great, great, great grand-daughter of the train robber and killer, Jesse James. I'm not sure if that's the right number of "greats", by the way. I always figured that her do-gooder instinct was driven in some way by a desire to make up for all of Jesse's thievin' and killin'. As far as I know, she never settled down with another man after we split up, so I always considered myself truly privileged to have been her only husband. I must have been quite a catch back then, although I like to think that I still am today and that my current wife, Billie-Jo, agrees with that.

Anyhow, I'm clearly jabberin' on – I probably shouldn't have had the six beers and three whores before I got here. The extra beer was just plain greedy. Still, I'm mighty impressed with the low prices since the ***Vegas drain*** stole most of your custom and livelihood. Oh, shit, there I go again, sayin' things that ain't gonna make me popular. I'll just get on with my poetry, so here goes…

This tale is known as "The Legend of Annie James". It's about the time that Annie tracked down the outlaw, Bobby-Ray Butcher, who was renowned for havin' the deepest voice of all the cowboys that ever roamed the desert plains. Annie said that his voice was deeper than the Pacific and had more rasp than sandpaper. It was as if the Devil himself was tryin' to speak from Bobby-Ray's throat. And it wasn't the only thing that he was known for…

Somethin' wicked…

Bounty Hunter I:
The Legend of Annie James

*A lady known to some folk as
"The Bravest Woman in the West"*

The bravest woman in the West was my wife, Annie James.
She lived her life beyond the edge, ensurin' fun and games.
But I was awful proud of Annie – glad to be her spouse.
She hunted outlaws, hangin' "Wanted" posters 'round the house.
Her face was marked with several scars from carrying out her duty,
but I could see beneath 'em. She was still my flame-haired beauty.

All heroes need a villain to bring out their gallant best,
and villains come in plentiful supply throughout the West.
A rumour started circulatin' of a man condemned
in several towns for killin' with his evil band of men.
His name was Bobby-Ray, and every poster showed him grinnin'
from beneath a jaunty ladies' hat, and wearin' fancy linen.

Those lawless men were all transvestite killers with a grudge.
They'd slaughter any lawman, from a sheriff to a judge.
As Bobby rode beyond the canyons to the hills and mines,
his bearded tranny posse closely followed from behind.
Arrivin' at the outskirts of a town, men stared in shock,
not knowin' death was fast approachin' in a paisley frock.

Though dainty from a distance they were vicious scum and freaks.
My Annie left to track 'em down, which took her several weeks.
She galloped through the desert to the mountains, through the pines,
and found them in a town that stood beside the silver mines.
She knew she felt the weird respect that any woman feels
for men adept at ridin' horses wearin' platform heels.

It wouldn't pay to underestimate those callous males
just because they roamed the West with painted fingernails.
As Annie rode into the town she saw the bodies lyin',
and women stooped beside 'em who were sick with grief and cryin'.
She heard some shots that seemed to come from more than one location.
She guessed the gang had split, and made the jail her destination.

The sheriff had been cornered there by headman, Bobby-Ray,
who gruffly told him, "Sheriff, go ahead and make my day.
Just tell me - honest as you can - d'you like me in this dress?"
The sheriff said, "Hell no, you goddamn queer, you look a mess!"
Well, Bobby yelled, "You think I'm queer, but I don't care. I ain't!
But I'm real pissed that you don't like my dress. I think it's quaint."

So Bobby fired his guns and filled the lawman full o' lead,
then wrapped a feather boa 'round the sheriff lyin' dead.
And that's the point that Annie entered, seein' Bobby-Ray,
his guns still smokin' in his handbag, proof of his foul play.
He opened up his parasol and turned to face my Annie.
He said, "Hey babe, I'm Bobby-Ray, but you can call me Fanny."

Rogue in a robe in a rage

My Annie told him straight, "Come quiet, or else you'll end up hurt",
but Bobby's face showed anger, as she wore a nicer skirt.
He didn't like to be upstaged and envy filled his eyes.
He whipped a gun out in a flash to hasten her demise.
But she drew faster, knowin' that was how she might survive
and Bobby-Ray was worth the same if dead or caught alive.

As Bobby's body bucked against the wall, then slid right down,
he stared at crimson blood and asked her, "Does it match my gown?"
She told him, "You're a bastard, feared in every town and city,
but as you draw your final breath, I'd say you still look pretty".
He briefly smiled, then passed away more pleased than he deserved,
and Annie took his skin cream, as his face looked well-preserved.

She headed to the clothin' store as, rightly, she'd surmised
a few of Bobby's men were tryin' skirts and slips for size.
Her guns a-blazin', blood and bras and panties filled the air.
She killed 'em all, then left, with bloomers sittin' on her hair.
With half the gang now fallen she would find the rest, she swore,
and tracked 'em by the body count up to the jeweller's store.

The owner dead, the men tried jewellery on in countless styles;
the finest silver bracelets, chains and earrings found for miles.
They shrieked and swapped their necklaces, then stuffed them in a sack,
and failed to notice Annie creepin' up behind their back.
She fired a single shot in warnin', causin' them to freeze,
and told 'em all to raise their hands and drop down to their knees.

But Bobby's men weren't gonna let some woman steal their plunder.
One man ran, but three remained whose weapons cracked like thunder.
A bullet punched a hole in Annie's arm, but not before
she'd pierced the hearts of all three men, who crashed upon the floor.
The one who'd sprinted off was clamberin' up onto his steed,
but Annie's bullet grazed his cheek before he fled at speed.

He must have felt relief, as blood dripped on his blouse and bra,
as Annie rarely missed her target, even from afar.
Still, she was pleased when she got back. She'd earned a decent bounty
and knew her reputation was the best in every county.
And so she dropped the bombshell that she needed to be free
and told me, though it grieved her, she was now divorcin' me.

I understood and signed the papers, keen to dodge a battle.
To help me cope with losin' her, I turned to rustlin' cattle.
And that's why I saw Annie next, a poster in her fist,
that bore my handsome face. She warned me, "Randy, don't resist!
I'm gonna have to take you in – you'll probably get a fine.
I think it's most unlikely that you'll end up doin' time."

Outlaws gettin' dressed to kill

Bounty Hunter II: The Rough Justice of Arnold Pecker

From a live performance at The Horseshoe Club casino, Reno, Nevada, during Jackson's "A Horse Called Stan" tour, 8 May 1994.

I sure wish Annie had been right. She was one of those women blessed with an optimistic disposition, which I always thought was strange when you consider the awful crimes and evil ways of the outlaws she was dealin' with, day after day.

I suppose she knew a lot about crimes as well as their punishment so, based on her belief, I guess I was also expectin' a fine at the most, especially considerin' it was my first offence. Well - the first I'd ever been caught for.

I was held for a few days in the local jail, as we didn't have a permanent judge of our own. We did at one time, called Justice Matlock, but he'd gotten himself in trouble over his fondness for erotic paintings, mostly shipped over from a goddamn effeminate place called Paris in France. In my opinion, it was *pornography* thinly disguised as art – but ain't that often the case!

I remember bein' in the public gallery once, while Matlock was sentencin' a petty thief for stealin' the swing doors from the latrine of the "Tickled Beaver" saloon. How he thought he'd get away with that durin' openin' hours was truly mystifyin'. The poor fella sittin' on the latrine at the time got one hell of a shock. Anyhow, watchin' the thief bein' sentenced while the Justice, in all his fine clothin' and horsehair wig, sat there with his latest piece of art hangin' on the wall behind him, was kinda odd. From where I was sittin', the picture looked like six naked ladies queuin' up in front of a mighty pleased-lookin' donkey, who had a string o' French onions around his neck and a French beret coverin' up his johnson. Apparently it was a metaphor for makin' the most of your days before life made an ass of you.

Anyhow, a time came when news reached Justice Matlock of a huge shipment of Parisian paintings bein' transported by rail to San Francisco. The judge couldn't afford to buy the whole collection, so he staged a railroad robbery and got caught. No one was killed durin' the robbery, but there was a lotta concern that, if Matlock wasn't punished severely, the Parisians might stop supplyin' their fancy perfumes to our whores. That would have caused quite a stink throughout the West and so, to avoid a public outcry, they hanged him.

Unfortunately, with the porn-lovin' judge arrested and hanged, I had to wait for the temporary Justice to arrive. And when he did, things turned out a lot more complicated than Annie had imagined. I sure wish she'd hung around but, Annie bein' Annie, she'd gone straight off to hunt down some other villain, leavin' me alone to face the consequences of my crimes. And that's where we pick up on the tale, with the second part of the story...

Bounty Hunter II:
The Rough Justice of Arnold Pecker

A man known to some folk as
"The Harshest Judge in the West"

The meanest judge that ever lived was sent to judge my case,
whose verdicts were unsparing if he didn't like your face.
And sometimes bein' innocent would draw the harshest sentence
for wastin' Justice Pecker's time, unless you showed repentance.
The jury found me guilty. Justice Pecker tweaked his wart
and said that I deserved to perish, just for bein' caught.

I'd never met a man with so much hatred in his heart.
He sentenced me to hang, because I clearly wasn't smart.
The news of judgement on my case reached Annie far away.
She galloped through the mountains and the canyons night and day
until she made it to my hometown, known as Carter's Bluff,
where I was bein' taken to the gallows in the buff.

That twisted judge had said I'd pay for sheer ineptitude
by endin' my days hangin' from a rope entirely nude.
My time was runnin' out as Annie raced across the square
and headed to the courthouse, as the judge was sittin' there.
She pleaded for my life, but knew the bastard hadn't listened,
then noticed, underneath his wig, a silver earring glistened.

A memory came back; his cheek was scarred, which reinforced it.
She'd watched him flee on horseback in a blouse and whalebone corset.
The judge was a transvestite, and the last of Bobby's gang.
She marched him to the gallows where I stood, about to hang.
My neck was in the noose, a trapdoor underneath my heels,
with seconds till it opened and no time for last appeals.

But Annie pushed the judge onto the platform by my side
and swapped the noose that looped my neck to his, and beamed with pride.
She said, "Hey, Randy, you look good - all naked, bound and gagged.
I'm pleased to let you know that for your age, not much has sagged."
She asked ol' Justice Pecker if he had one last request.
He begged her to be kind enough to fetch his Sunday best.

He told us that a special day demanded somethin' fittin'
and slipped into a pleated skirt and shawl that he'd been knittin'.
He took a breath and thanked us, then removed his horsehair wig.
The door beneath his feet gave way. He danced a final jig.
I think it was a square-dance, though it's mighty hard to tell.
His buckin' corpse was smilin' as his soul returned to hell.

I would have raised my hat to Annie, as the townsfolk watched,
but kept it where it was, as it was coverin' my crotch.
Besides I didn't want to lead the ladies to temptation,
in case a stampede started that could swamp the elevation.
A massive cheer went up for Annie as she rode away,
while I received a pardon, and a very nice bouquet.

Just desserts for Justice Pecker

Lady Jane

From a live performance at Fort Lewis College campus, Durango, Colorado, during Jackson's "Brink o' Death" tour, 17 December 2005.

Before we get much further, I wanted to say to you that I feel mighty honoured to be visitin' your fine, multi-cultural college and spendin' this time with you, as I didn't get much of an opportunity for formal education myself. I reckon there ain't one of you older than twenty-two. At your age, I'd have been more interested in hikin' into the beautiful mountains 'round here - in the hope o' makin' out with some young lady - instead of sittin' here, listenin' to an old cowboy yammerin' on. I guess you can do that later. In fact, I'd recommend it. I think relaxin' in your mineral springs this afternoon, along with the clean mountain air, has gone and roused me up beyond the appropriate.

Anyhow, I've been told that some of my tales from times past, which are stories from my own and other people's lives, have some real educational value and are even on your history curriculum. I guess I owe you all an apology for that. [Laughter]. No. I was bein' serious. [Laughter]. No. Really. Gee - I just don't get young people sometimes.

But I was particularly pleased to hear that the core parts of my work that you study are the tales of the legendary Annie James. So you'll all be familiar with the time she tracked down the vicious transvestite killer known as Bobby-Ray Butcher and his gang. Now Annie kept in touch with me for a long time after we divorced. I'd get letters from all over, and this is one she sent me soon after she'd caught those outlaws. Let me read it to you (and I'll try and get her voice right). It says:

"Hi Randy. I sure miss the feel of your whiskery face against my thighs, although not the rash it used to give me. I've been makin' a fortune off my reputation since capturing the Butcher gang. The Wild West feels a whole lot safer with Bobby-Ray out of the picture, that's for sure.

"One thing I found out that I thought you'd find interestin' is that those tranny fellas were all born and raised by the women of Skull Creek. I remember you talkin' about the place once, and it's the only time I ever saw you get twitchy like that. I hope you've got over those bad dreams you used to have about the place. I have to tell you; even I wouldn't rush to Skull Creek for a fistful of dollars. Just as well there's no shortage of robbers and killers elsewhere.

"I expect you've found a new lady by now, but hope you still think of me from time to time. I also hope I didn't bruise your big cowboy heart too bad. I guess your horse, Stanley, is doin' okay too? Love. Annie"

Well, of course, I did still think of my Annie, but she was one of many colourful characters back then. I'd like to tell you about another couple of equally fascinating folks, the first bein' a woman known as "Lady Jane".

Lady Jane

A lady known to some folk as
"The Wildest Woman in the West"

It took a posse, fit and strong, to carry Lady Jane,
ejectin' her from the saloon. She cussed and kicked in vain.
Her teeth were missin' at the front from scraps with other men,
and tufts o' hair were torn out fightin' ladies now'n' again.
Jane had the fiercest temper in the West beyond a doubt
and she was ugly as a bulldog; face all twisted up to shout.

Some girls make up with inner beauty, knockin' men out flat.
And what I noticed most in Jane was – she had none o' that!
She swore so much I knew that she was cursed or badly bred.
I don't know why I married her. I must have lost my head.
I guess I felt electric sparks fly every time she passed
that made my hair stand upright – and my johnson followed fast!

I still recall our wedding day, before our weddin' feast;
she knocked out several choirboys, kicked my horse, then punched the priest.
Though why my horse was in the church, I'm stumped, but someone said
they thought he hoped to rescue me from Jane before we wed.
Our wedding night was passionate; Jane knew no holdin' back.
She hollered loudly, wakin' half the town when in the sack

One time I covered up her mouth to quieten her in bed.
She deeply bit three fingers – left one hangin' by a thread.
I never made the same mistake again – just let her scream.
She even cussed when fast asleep, fists flailin' as she dreamed.
I got so many black eyes people thought I loved to brawl,
as cowboys learn to fight as babes, before they talk or crawl.

The townsfolk had enough of Jane and said she'd have to go.
I broke the news as gently as I could, but feared she'd blow.
I wasn't wrong. She ran into the square and dared them all
to take her on in unarmed combat, cravin' flesh to maul.
But while she shouted, someone crept behind with a lasso
and tied her to my horse and whipped his butt till off he flew.

Though frankly I don't think my horse had needed much persuadin'.
He dragged her through the dirt for miles, a-huffin' and a-brayin'.
He looked so pleased when he got back, and what was left of Jane
I buried in three baked bean cans near Utah, on the plain.
I wonder if she leaves her grave and stalks that town at night
to whisper in the ears of men to make them brawl and fight.

I think I mostly felt relieved. I saddled up my horse
and left for new adventures, glad for such a cheap divorce.
So if you're ever roamin' through the Southwest desert plains
and find a cactus twisted like a rabid beast in pain,
beneath it, by a headstone, is the place Jane lies at rest.
Don't shed a tear, just yell a curse. I think she'd like that best.

Lady Jane tangles with Stanley

The Fountain

From a live performance at Fort Lewis College campus, Durango, Colorado, during Jackson's "Brink o' Death" tour, 17 December 2005.

I thought you'd like Lady Jane. That was a true story, by the way. She was my ninth wife. Nine was always my lucky number till I met her, on account of me bein' born on the ninth of the ninth, ninety-nine. That's the 9th September 1899 to those of you who struggle with math. I guess that makes me – jeez – old enough to be most of your great-grand-pappies. [Applause]

No, dammit! Don't clap just for me gettin' old. I hate it when folk do that – clappin' every time some ol' fogey tells you their age. Gets me all riled up. Why the hell d'you think I called it the "Brink o' Death" tour anyhow? While I'm here, I've a good mind to head off skiin' for the weekend in your mountain resort. They call it Purgatory, am I right?

[Laughter]. You doubt this ol' fossil can ski? You should see me in my chaps and spurs on a snowboard. I'd challenge any one of you to race me on the powder of your toughest piste. I'll beat the fittest of you and that's a promise – even you sir, with the six-pack and tree-trunk thighs. I reckon it's my continuin' zest for life and adventure that's keepin' me lookin' – let's be generous – fifty years younger than I am. [Laughter]

That laughter sure makes me nervous. Ha. Back in the late sixties I did a tour I called the "Alimony" comeback tour, as some of my wives were forcin' me to bankroll their twilight years. I've outlasted most of 'em now, which is why I've mostly quit tourin'. I don't need the dollars.

But I promised you another tale, though I should mention there's some adult content comin' your way. In fact, the only time I previously stopped tourin', durin' the height of my fame, was when I told this next tale to a convention of church ministers, which damn near killed off my career in the early '80s. When I finally got goin' again, it was my wife, Billie-Jo, who persuaded me to change the name of the tour from the "Fuck You, Padre" tour to somethin' less provocative. But I'm guessin' these are more enlightened times and you folk are plenty broadminded enough. That's what I like about young people so much. It's like when they say, "A pet ain't just for Christmas". I've always said, "A young person ain't just for makin' love to." Though it's nice.

Anyhow, the poem that follows is about a fella called Billy. I've changed a line in the first stanza for my own amusement and hopefully yours, to give it a modern twist. But this tale, in truth, goes back to the early 1900s when I was just a boy, and it comes from a place near the town where I was raised. There's an unnamed villain in the piece and I never did manage to find out his name, but like most of the godforsaken things in my life, I did discover that he allegedly came from Skull Creek. Shit! I can see your Principal at the back of the hall shakin' his head and gesturin', so I'm gonna get on before he tries to stop me...

The Fountain

A tale known to some folk as
"The Ballad of Buggering Billy"

As a kid he frolicked with the young boys in the fountain,
and growin' up he learned the facts of life from Brokeback Mountain.
He roughly wrestled wranglers all throughout his teenage years
and when they yelled "Enough!" and cried, would softly wipe their tears.
He knew to hide from friends he loved the depth of his devotion;
men as prickly as cacti and as sparing of emotion.
He made the most of jostling with the roughnecks at the bar;
enjoyed their scent of honest toil on ranch and fields afar.

It must be said that Billy had some brushes with the law,
but unlike other cowboys never slept with any whore.
One day a handsome stranger stopped at Billy's for the night.
A widowed lady spied on them and fainted at the sight.
For Billy had a gift for spottin' men, just passin' by,
who'd take more than a stogey offered by a willing guy.
Word spread around and Billy soon was shunned at each saloon.
Beth, the brothel pianist, refused to play his favourite tune.

For others, life was hard but good. The men were mighty brave;
until one day a villain sent the strongest to their grave.
The townsfolk lived in fear – were forced to offer up their wives
who kicked and screamed, but soon complied, to save their husbands' lives.
One day that scoundrel picked on Billy, actin' kinda tough.
Billy raised an eyebrow, then a fist. He liked it rough.
The villain punched with evil blows that made an awful sound,
but Billy grabbed and lifted him, then threw him to the ground.

He ripped the villain's chaps apart, and yanked his pants right down
and buggered him from dusk till dawn in front of half the town.
The good folk gathered, cheerin', pleased to hear the varmint's shrieks.
He left the town for good that day, remainin' sore for weeks.
Hank, the local sculptor, made a statue of that scene
and placed it in the fountain in the town square to be seen.
That monument to victory made the townsfolk mighty proud
and everyone loved Billy and would call his name aloud.

The only slight confusion for the kids, which stopped their shoutin',
was tryin' to suss the statue's pose while splashin' in the fountain,
except for little Tommy, the adopted son of Billy.
He sure loved spurs and leatherwear - and found those cowboys pretty.
That boy grew up with tolerance that fostered self-expression.
Yeah, Billy taught those people well to stand against oppression.
And once a year, without their wives, the menfolk went away
to pair up in the woods to re-enact that special day.

"I'm just headin' out to the woods right now myself
if any of you fine young fellas want to tag along..."

- Randall J. Jackson

Sculptor Hank's *Monument to Victory*

The Scarecrow Maker

From a live performance at The Silver Dollar Bar hotel, Jackson Hole, Wyoming, during Jackson's "How to Barbecue a Mongoose" tour, 15 July 1981.

Howdy fellas. Ladies. My name's Randall J. Jackson, but you can call me Randy. I expect you've heard the trouble I had a week or so back, when I performed for a bunch of chaplains, ministers and priests at their convention in Sedona, Arizona. I love the way that sounds, by the way, don't you? *Sedona, Arizona.* Quite by accident, I unintentionally recited a poem that they thought endorsed and encouraged the act of sodomy. Well, I can tell you, when I saw the way they shiftily glanced sideways at their companions as I recited the poem, it was clear to me that they didn't need much encouragement. As a result though, this tour is stoppin' short, as most venues have cancelled on me, and you're the last folk to hear it. I sure hope I manage to avoid offendin' anyone here.

So! I've arrived in the heart and soul of Jackson Hole at your fine establishment. Incidentally, this town isn't named after me – or any part of me – in case you were wonderin'.

I understand you've only just reopened after a few problems of your own. Who'd have thought a bird could be stupid enough to nest on a hotel roof right by an electrical transformer. I salute your hard work at gettin' the place up and runnin' again after it virtually burnt to the ground less than a year ago. You can imagine the thoughts goin' through the birdbrains of those tiny chicks as they hatched and looked up at their mother: Hey, mommy, what are those sparks doin' flyin over our home, is there a firework display nearby? Hey, mommy, why's there smoke comin' off your tail feathers? Hey, mommy, little Milly hasn't hatched yet, and she's gettin' kinda poached. Hey mommy, you smell of barbecue. [SILENCE]

I guess that's not too amusin'. Sorry. I seem to be sufferin' from a lack of good judgement these days. Anyhow, one thing I've noticed that's changed since I last stayed here is the menu in the restaurant. You don't seem to be servin' bird's nest soup anymore. [SILENCE]

O-kay. Let's stick to the poetry. I thought I'd share a piece about one of my wives. As you know, I've been married many times, sometimes more successfully than others. I know I don't look it, but I'm eighty-one years old. That means I've already outlived a number of my wives, includin' Katie, who this poem's about. When I went to get her death certificate from the coroner I found out one fact that, probably, in retrospect, shouldn't have surprised me at all. I don't know why I'd never found this out while we were together and she was alive. But it turned out that Kate was born in Skull Creek. Well, if you've followed my work at all, you'll know that Skull Creek has been a bad omen that, one way or another, has dogged me most of my days. Those two little words have been a dark shadow loomin' over my life. Perhaps that explains some of what follows.

The Scarecrow Maker

A woman known to some folk as "Neurotic Katie"

My fifteenth wife was Katie. She found man and beast repulsive.
She was manically depressive and obsessively compulsive.
She gave me latex gloves to wear and screwed her face uptight
if we were walkin' hand in hand or makin' love at night.
I felt my ardour dwindle in the face of her disgust.
She'd chase an airborne speck o' dirt before it lay as dust
and polish both her nipples till they glinted in the sun,
but wouldn't let me tweak 'em, with her allergy to fun.

Like many wives before her, she developed deep mistrust
of Stan, my trusty steed, who she refused to ride or touch.
She claimed that Stan was filthy in his cloud of flies – and germy!
But he was more afraid of her. She practised taxidermy.
Our ranch was full of critters Kate had caught and badly stuffed,
whose fear-filled eyes were wide with shock - and clearly less than chuffed.
They'd met their maker in cruel hands that loved to kill and pluck -
left starin' like Joan Rivers after one more nip 'n' tuck.

It was best to stay in motion – standin' still near Kate for long
would capture her attention, armed with scissors and a prong.
One time, after a lunchtime drink, returnin' to our home
I noticed Stan, my horse, was lookin' crazed - mouth full o' foam.
Now Stan was kinda greedy and his stack of hay was gone.
I'd warned him not to be a pig, but his appetite was strong.
Had indigestion left that strained expression on his face?
No. Kate had stuffed him from both ends. That look was fixed in place.

I should've told the sheriff what she'd done but froze with fright,
as she was armed with cuttin' tools and cacklin' with delight.
I gave her one more chance despite my stallion's sad demise.
She cleaned up neat – obsessively – and to my great surprise
she didn't leave a trace. She swept the yard and mopped the floor,
then washed her hands for several days until she'd rubbed 'em raw.
She seemed to change her ways, so I relaxed, enjoyin' life.
We settled into staid routines like any man and wife.

I would work and buy our food, while she'd wash clothes and cook.
And evenings we'd sit by the fire and read a favourite book.
Sometimes my buddies, Frank and Jesse, came to socialise.
One evening, I ran out of beer and went for fresh supplies.
When I returned, my friends appeared much fatter than before.
My Kate had whipped their insides out and filled 'em full o' straw.
I couldn't find her anywhere but tried to track her down.
Her tools were gone and strange sights greeted me about the town.

A granny darnin' socks seemed awful still upon her stool.
Three kids were propped on bicycles against a stable wall.
The carpenter was at his bench. His handheld saw was frozen.
He gazed at wood he'd halfway cut, eyes shocked but lackin' motion.
And by his feet and also stickin' from his pants and sleeves
were tufts o' straw. No wonder he was lookin' mighty peeved.
My angst was risin' fast, so I increased my stridin' pace,
but everywhere I searched I found another rigid face.

A local wrangler stiffly stood beside a wooden fence.
Behind him, cattle tamely stared, bemused, yet somehow tense.
As I approached, they failed to move or make a livin' sound.
Their udders pointed everywhere, except towards the ground.
A mother hangin' washin' out nearby seemed paralysed.
She stared with fright at skid-marked drawers that clearly weren't her size.
Had she been alive I would have helped her feel much prouder
by advisin' her to switch to "Daz" – a better washin' powder.

I tapped an old man's shoulder standin' by the general store
in case he'd seen my wife. He swayed - then toppled to the floor.
And in a neighbour's yard a muzzled dog known for aggression
stood like a statue, leg cocked high, and bore a stunned expression.
My Kate had turned to killin' like some creepy scarecrow-maker.
You'd think that she'd been sponsored by the local undertaker.
I bumped into the sheriff followin' the trail o' straw.
We'd both gone 'round in circles as it led back to my door.

We found Kate in the basement, beamin' like some evil elf,
but hay was pokin' from her ears. She'd gone and stuffed herself!
Her dyin' wish was written down, but left me quite dismayed.
She'd left her body to the town and wanted it displayed.
We checked with the museum but they showed us to the door
as Kate was last seen filleting their cherished dinosaur.
That beast was their prized specimen and mummified intact,
but padded out with straw grinned like a startled artefact.

It's just as well Kate left a note explainin' what she'd done
or I'd have been convicted for her crimes and swiftly hung.
In truth, the sheriff questioned me in jail, and left me sweatin'.
I faced his accusation I'd been aidin' and abettin',
but evidence was circumstantial. Legal folk agreed.
And all potential witnesses were stuffed, so I was freed.
Now Katie's corpse stands by my bed and, fitted with a shade,
she makes a lovely bedroom lamp, but scares the chambermaid.

"I'm mighty glad that she was the only serial killer I ever married."
– Randall J. Jackson

Taxidermist, Katie, *gettin' stuffed!*

Angels of Matrimony

From a rare overseas live performance at The Royal Albert Hall, London, England, during Jackson's "The Many Wives of Randall J. Jackson" tour, 26 June 2002.

My eighteenth wife, Billie-Jo, persuaded me to see a therapist once, at a time when psychology and other newfangled ideas, such as rules and regulations about equality, diversity and other shit, reached the West.

The guy I saw was a Chinese psychotherapist, called Dr. Wan Ka-Ching. It was nothin' to do with my philanderin' ways; Billie-Jo was more concerned about my state of mind when my bad dreams started plaguing me again. I called them my "Skull Creek flashbacks".

Dr. Ka-Ching was of the opinion that I wanted to sleep with my own mother, but once I'd talked him out of that notion he confessed that it was actually his desire. I had to give him a hug he was cryin' so much, but after that we started to make some progress. I think I helped the funny little fella a lot – but he sure charged me a lot for his emotional development.

At first, he didn't believe me when I told him that I'd been married eighteen times, and I had to write all their names down in the poem I'm about to share with you to persuade him I was tellin' the truth. Dr. Ka-Ching had some major trust issues. He'd often get his bible out and make me swear on oath that I was bein' honest with him. Again, I think I helped him deal with his suspicion and paranoia issues, even though it cost me many hundreds o' dollars.

He was equally stunned when I explained that I had no children from all of my marriages, and I suppose it was kinda odd. But by some weird quirk o' fate, each and every one of my wives was infertile. Now I don't much believe in God or have any time for religion, but a number of my wives, well, they remarried after we split up. And every one that did – they conceived their first children within a few months of bein' with their new partners. Now that's what I call a miracle! Enough to make a man believe. Almost.

Dr. Ka-Ching thought he could help, and gave me some herbs to rub around my johnson before makin' love to increase both mine and Billie-Jo's fertility. I wouldn't have minded but, unfortunately, he'd got his pills and potions muddled up, and it turned out that the herbs he'd given me were stingin' nettles. I wasn't best pleased.

I tried to tell him about my "Skull Creek flashbacks", which were the reason I'd become his patient in the first place, but he'd just say, "is very, very bad place" and refuse to talk about it. He was clearly *in avoidance* of the subject and asked me if I could give him some marital advice instead. So I told him about my wives again, as I'm about to tell you….

Angels of Matrimony

***The ladies known to some folk as
"The 18 Blessed Wives of Randy Jackson"***

My first wife was Susannah, though they called her Windy Sue.
One time, she cleared the general store by lettin' off a brew.
She glared at me to pass the blame, while folk ran for the door,
but I was in the danger zone and fainted to the floor.
My second wife was Trudy, always seekin' out attention.
She nearly got me killed with pranks requirin' intervention.
Once, while Jed, my friend and wranglin' partner, sorted feed,
among the hungry cattle Trudy started a stampede.

She'd opened up a cage of angry rattlers that we'd caught
and set 'em free among the cows who soon became distraught.
I tried to help on horseback, ridin' Stan, the bravest steed,
but he was scared of snakes, so threw me off and fled at speed.
As poundin' hooves were raisin' storms of dust that hid the ground,
I dived into the water trough with Jed and nearly drowned.
My third wife, Sally, mostly liked to flirt with rougher men,
and loved to end up roughly handled - by the most o' them!

Then Pixie came along and, though petite, she moved like lightnin'.
She'd won some trophies as a champ at men's bare knuckle fightin'.
Away from contests, Pixie was as gentle as a mouse.
One time, I was away, and three intruders stalked the house.
They woke her up in bed, and their intentions weren't too nice.
She asked them all to leave, but they ignored her good advice.
When I came back, I thought I'd had too many at the bar
as, in the fridge, three pickled johnsons floated in a jar.

But when it came to bravery, my Annie beat the rest.
She'd built her reputation catchin' villains of the West.
She trapped a gang of robbers once, who plagued the richest towns
and stormed the banks on unicycles, dressed as circus clowns.
But Annie caught 'em, using clever games instead of force,
by hidin' at the rear end of their getaway panto horse.
The thieves stood on the saddle in a pyramid formation,
and as they fled she steered them straight towards the sheriff's station.

Then Daisy was my sixth wife, who I loved despite her flaws
and wooden body parts - her death left weepin' sores.
A close friend, Buck, consoled me when she died, to ease my strife.
He held me close and hugged me; then became my seventh wife.
We got on well as man to man, until the fateful day
I knew I'd have to leave him when he told me he was gay.
My eighth, an Indian squaw called Flame, had scalps around her belt
belonging to ex-husbands who'd insulted her, she felt.

I have to say I handled our divorce with utmost care
determined to release myself while keepin' all my hair.
I thought she was a Navaho, but she claimed Cherokee.
She scalped me by the courthouse when the Justice set me free.
I sure was glad the surgeon came in time to sew it back
and someone pinned her down as she was goin' for my sac!
Jane came next - the ninth - and wildest woman in the West.
She carved our names and date we met with knives upon my chest.

I used a lonely-hearts club based in Vegas to decide
if anyone could follow Jane to be my latest bride.
Everything was done by post – assistin' love to bloom
with weddin' rings exchanged in letters coated with perfume.
And that's how I found Tammy, who I met after we'd wed.
She turned up on my doorstep to enjoy my marriage bed,
but towering two feet over me, she'd mis-described herself.
When I looked straight ahead at her, I hypnotised myself.

I took some pals to Vegas to annul the postal vows,
but I was told the deed was valid, as the law allows.
It's just as well, in Vegas, a divorce is twice as fast,
and then the boys and I went gamblin', havin' quite a blast.
I got so drunk that, for amusement, Jesse, Frank and Jed
all thought they'd set me up again, and try to get me wed.
I woke up feelin' hazy, in a scuzzy motel room,
and heard the snores from somethin' big beside me in the gloom.

I started feelin' nervous, as I wore a brand new ring.
I tried hard to remember but could not recall a thing.
I turned towards the weight that strained the mattress by my side,
and pulled aside the veil that covered up my sleepin' bride.
Big brown eyes popped open and a huge tongue licked my face.
The beast was Stan, my stallion, who was takin' all the space.
I kissed him I felt such relief, although I felt like death,
but Stan recoiled in horror from my stagnant mornin' breath.

He rolled out of the bed and huffed, then bolted through the door.
I wondered how we'd spent the night, as I was feelin' sore.
I had a break from marriage till I met number eleven.
She was such a peach, I thought I'd died and gone to heaven.
Her name was Molly Day and all the fellas found her stunnin',
until she opened up her mouth and shrieked, which sent 'em runnin'.
Her voice, like diamonds scrapin' glass, could unblock stubborn drains.
They banned her singin' hymns in church, for crackin' windowpanes.

Along came Tess, a pretty girl, to make up my first dozen.
We'd met as kids because she was my best friend Frank's half-cousin.
But Tess was real traditional and, though she liked to spoon,
refused to go much further till we reached our honeymoon.
I found her flaw the night we wed – quite rare in any lover –
that also, underneath the sheets, she was her own twin brother.
I guess I was annoyed with Frank who knew of her surprise.
He told me Tess, at school, could pee much higher than the guys.

But luck was fast approachin' in the shape of sweet thirteen;
the supple-jointed Sarah and my Midwest beauty queen.
She was a great contortionist and good at breakin' free
from any bonds or chains, but never flushed the lavatory.
It drove me mad. I'd tell her off, then take my seat, and find
her hand had slithered up the S-bend, slappin' my behind.
The fourteenth on my list of love was Sophie, struck with envy.
A single glance at any lady drove her to a frenzy.

One time she saw me talkin' to a girl and when I kissed her,
refused to trust my earnest claim that she was just my sister.
I couldn't understand why jealous Sophie went so wild.
I guess I must have told her once that I'm an only child.
My fifteenth wife was Kate, who kept stuffed varmints in the chiller -
a skilful taxidermist who became a serial killer.
She stuffed poor Frank and Jesse, who I left with her a while,
and now they're both in storage with an unconvincin' smile.

Ruth came next who people thought both stubborn and strong willed,
but I was grievin' for my friends and horse, who Kate had killed.
Ruth's violent sneezin' habit made kids cry with real distress.
I even dyed my hair green to disguise the sprayed-on mess.
Then brothel madam, Heidi, was my seventeenth - a beauty.
But I could never see a whore while Heidi was on duty.
That's mighty inconvenient, as all cowboys need their passion,
and I was never used to livin' off a meagre ration.

But Heidi got into my heart by trackin' down the twin
of Stan, my horse, and bought him as a gift, which made me grin.
I named him Stan, just like the first, and everything was swell,
though Heidi sprayed him with perfume to hide his pungent smell.
I felt so happy; I stopped cheatin' like some goddamn sneak
behind my Heidi's back, which almost lasted for a week.
You'd think a brothel madam would be used to manly ways,
but Heidi soon divorced me - after barely twenty days!

I lost myself in whiskey bars and ridin' rodeo,
and that's where I found love to last when I met Billie-Jo.
We fought like cat and dog at first, as she was full o' fire
and both of us were bossy, filled with lust and raw desire.
She asked me how I knew she'd cheated with the blacksmith, Ryan,
but I could see he'd scorched her buttocks with his brandin' iron.
I've learnt a lot from wives and friends and many tough divorces,
but mostly, I'd say never share a bed with frisky horses.

ADVERTISEMENT

Attract the Right Kind o' Woman...

Smell Like A Cowboy

WANTED!

The Original Scent of The Wild West

Try our new "Wanted: Hints"
Eau de Toilette range:

WANTED:	**WANTED:**
RODEO	**RIPE**
A Hint of Bronco	**A Hint of Armpit**

The Taming of Randy

From a live performance at Furnace Creek Inn, Death Valley, California, during Jackson's "Desert Demons" tour, 15 February 1973.

Demons come in all shapes and sizes. I even thought my current wife – and she hates it when I call her that – was a bit of a demon herself when I first married her. But we've been together almost forty years now. There's also a twelve-year age gap between me and Billie-Jo, which is why she's still so stunnin' to my eyes, despite the fact that I'm personally gettin' a bit wrinkly in quite a number of places, I don't mind tellin' you.

Billie-Jo's daddy had been a gold rush pioneer and made a fortune from buyin' up land and diggin' out the hills like a goddamn human gold detector. As a result, she had big expectations of the men in her life and mostly found disappointment. I was able to provide her with more o' that too, and she was none too shy lettin' me know about it. She wanted fine jewellery and automobiles, but the whole of America was only just comin' out of the Great Depression when we met.

I remember my own daddy showin' me a photo of ol' Henry Ford's weird contraption, the automobile, when I was about five years old. My daddy said he'd have one o' those one day, but he never did, bless his soul. Even when I met Billie-Jo, there were only two fellas in my town that had automobiles, and the gas stations were few and far between. They'd head out on business in their strange vehicles and, if they misjudged things, we'd have to send out cans o' gas – you've guessed it – on horseback, to rescue them from the desert heat. So I wouldn't have been in any rush to own one, even if I'd had a stash o' dollars. The West was still wild where I was livin' and had a lotta catchin' up to do with the rest of America and all it's advances. The only thing a man could safely rely on back then was his horse and a few close buddies.

Billie-Jo's daddy had put his gold-minin' fortune into somethin' called the "stock market" over in New York and, come the Depression, lost everythin' he owned and had gone and hanged himself. So Billie-Jo was full o' anger and a fair helpin' of resentment at havin' to earn her own livin' when I met her. But she had more determination than a desert fox diggin' a jackrabbit out of its hole. I think that's one of three things I most admired about her. And you can guess the other two.

Over time, I taught Billie-Jo how to write poetry, and she's turned out to be a mighty fine poet herself. One of the first poems she ever wrote was about the time we first met. Back then, I was strugglin' to make money out of cattle ranchin', so I was also ridin' rodeo to try and earn enough to make ends meet. Billie-Jo breezed in as a union rep with a background in somethin' she called Human Resources – or "H.R." for short. Sounded like a pile o' horseshit to most of us fellas back then and – tell ya the truth – it still does today. But Billie-Jo had the balls to stand up to anyone and anythin'. I remember one time, a tornado whipped through town. Well, Billie-Jo was leavin' the hairdressers after spendin' half her monthly wage havin' her hair restyled. She must have gotten too damn close to the twister's funnel as it spiralled down Main Street - and it rearranged her hair a second time. She was none too pleased and chased right after it, out into the desert, yellin' and cursin' and shakin' her fists and darin' it to try that again. If I didn't know better, I'd swear the squealin' winds started screechin' even louder, as if the tornado was afraid of her. I kept a very low profile the rest o' that day, as it's kinda hard to tell your wife that her hair looks pretty when it's just been whisked up by a cyclone. I figured I might need to laugh – and it would probably be the last thing I ever did.

Anyhow… without further delay, I'd like to invite my wife, Billie-Jo, onto the stage to share the tale of our first meetin'. Billie-Jo thinks of it as a romantic piece but, to my recollection, I think of it as a nightmarish time. As always, we beg to differ, but you folk can make up your own mind. So please give her a big hand – my wife – Billie-Jo…

The Taming of Randy

A Tale of Romance and Equality
by Billie-Jo Jackson

I first saw Randy at the brothel door with a cigar,
but knew his reputation for the ladies and the bar.
I'd joined the local rodeo when H.R. reached the West,
though equal opportunities left cowboys unimpressed.
I faced some real resentment as a union rep, but tried
to get those cowboys to believe that I was on their side.

That's where I next saw Randy, dustin' off after a fall.
A cloven hoof had torn his pants and he was showin' all.
He cursed and spluttered till he saw me walkin' up to him.
He must have been good-lookin' once, despite his crooked grin.
I said, "Hey fella, I'm your rep. Instead of just complainin'
I think it's time you booked yourself some health and safety trainin'."

He slyly looked me up and down, both hands on his six-shooters,
and said, "Hey, pumpkin, you're a sight with lovely cowgirl hooters,
enough to make a cowboy smile and sweet as cotton-candy.
You're lucky that I'm free tonight – come home and romp with Randy."
While tempted, I sensed danger there, though single at the time.
But I was workin' late shift, tryin' to earn an honest dime.

Besides, he had a one-track mind and seventeen divorces,
and clearly liked to grapple with a girl's human resources.
Well, this girl wanted real respect, not tumbles in the hay.
I turned him down. He scratched his johnson, frownin' with dismay.
Yet mischief etched his face in lines, eyes sparklin' as he looked.
I tried to keep him from my mind. The rascal had me hooked.

He asked me out to dinner. I caved in under duress.
In truth, I was quite chuffed and wore my finest party dress.
I wondered what fine car would come to whisk me off at speed,
but what stood droppin' turd upon my drive was Randy's steed.
Still, Randy was the livin' proof that romance hadn't died.
The restaurant was exclusive – it served just Kentucky Fried.

It took some time to teach him manners; change his sexist ways
and learn some modern legislation for these modern days.
I wouldn't be the one to cook his every evenin' meal.
He'd take his turn if we were wed, 'cause that was half the deal.
I banned him from the brothels and late nights at the saloon.
We'd cuddle on the sofa watchin' westerns like "High Noon".

At Christmastime I let him smoke a single fine cigar.
I made him swap his bucktoothed stallion for a decent car.
He cried the day they took his horse, but I could not endure
the looks at every place we went for stinkin' like manure.
I made him grateful, reined him in, and whipped his cowboy hide.
I broke him like a buckin' bronco just to be his bride.

Then came the time we kissed goodnight I noticed, by the taste,
that he'd been kissin' someone else. Was I to be replaced?
He said, "Hey pumpkin, I have read your legislation fully.
The local judge agrees with me that you're a textbook bully.
By Western laws your bannin' me from brothels gives me fuel
to press for a divorce, as it's emotionally cruel".

Well, Randy had a point and I deserved to take some flack,
as I'd had twelve affairs in our first year, behind his back.
I'd given myself so much freedom I was feelin' trapped,
especially at the point when six affairs had overlapped.
Still, Randy was a sly and cheatin' bastard just like me.
That's why we stuck together, blessed with true equality.

The Wrath of Skull Creek

From a live performance at Furnace Creek Inn, Death Valley, California, during Jackson's "Desert Demons" tour, 15 February 1973.

Just so you know, although Billie-Jo did sell my horse, I bought him back and kept him hidden in the dilapidated ol' stable block at the furthest corner of my ranch. I'd lost Stan once when my serial-killin' taxidermist wife, Katie, stuffed him. I wasn't gonna lose him again now that I had him back in the form of his stallion twin, also named Stan.

My time in therapy with Dr. Wan Ka-Ching hadn't helped much with sortin' out my indecipherable "Skull Creek flashbacks". I told him that Billie-Jo reckoned somethin' had happened out there that was deeply buried in my sub-conscious mind and I was too afraid to remember. Every time I brought up the subject with Dr. Ka-Ching, he told me that he could hypnotise me to help me suppress the memory better. I didn't think that was the right approach, although I did continue with his herbal remedies and method of application to aid my fertility, hopin' to finally give Billie-Jo the son or daughter she'd always wanted.

Jed, my best friend, was finally talkin' to me again at that time. He'd been real pissed with me when Katie had also killed Frank and Jesse, as they were his friends too. I'd barely seen him for two years. But he still had fond memories of the frisky moments we used to share while tendin' cattle when we were young wranglin' dudes. He lived in constant hope of rekindlin' those moments, but it was only a passin' phase for me and just to help deal with the cold out on the desert plains on a bitter night. Billie-Jo liked Jed bein' around, as I only pestered her for love-makin' once a day, as I was exhausted from tryin' to keep Jed out of my pants.

Jed told me that, in his opinion, the only way I'd ever get over my "Skull Creek flashbacks" was by goin' back there and facin' my fears. It had been almost twenty years since I first passed through that infernal pit of damned souls, and I was vergin' on middle age now. Returnin' there didn't appeal to me much, as the place still had a reputation for spawnin' villains like some goddamn gateway from hell. But Jed said he'd come along and we could share a tent together to keep warm at rest stops on the way. I sometimes thought he was more cunnin' than a woman for settin' up situations to get into another man's chaps. He'd never had a wife or girlfriend, despite bein' almost as handsome as ol' Randy here. He got plenty of offers from the ladies all the same, and it left 'em mighty perplexed that they were doin' all the chasin' for no fun. I never understood how he could resist their charms when they were rubbin' their hooters against him for free, and he'd just carry on suppin' his beer.

Anyhow, that's how we found ourselves traipsin' across the red rock dustbowls of Arizona and Utah, headin' in the direction of the meanest place on Earth. But I also think Jed wanted payback on Skull Creek for Kate slaughterin' our friends, as she was born there. And whenever we rested, Jed was kind enough to help me apply Dr. Ka-Ching's herbal rub.

*

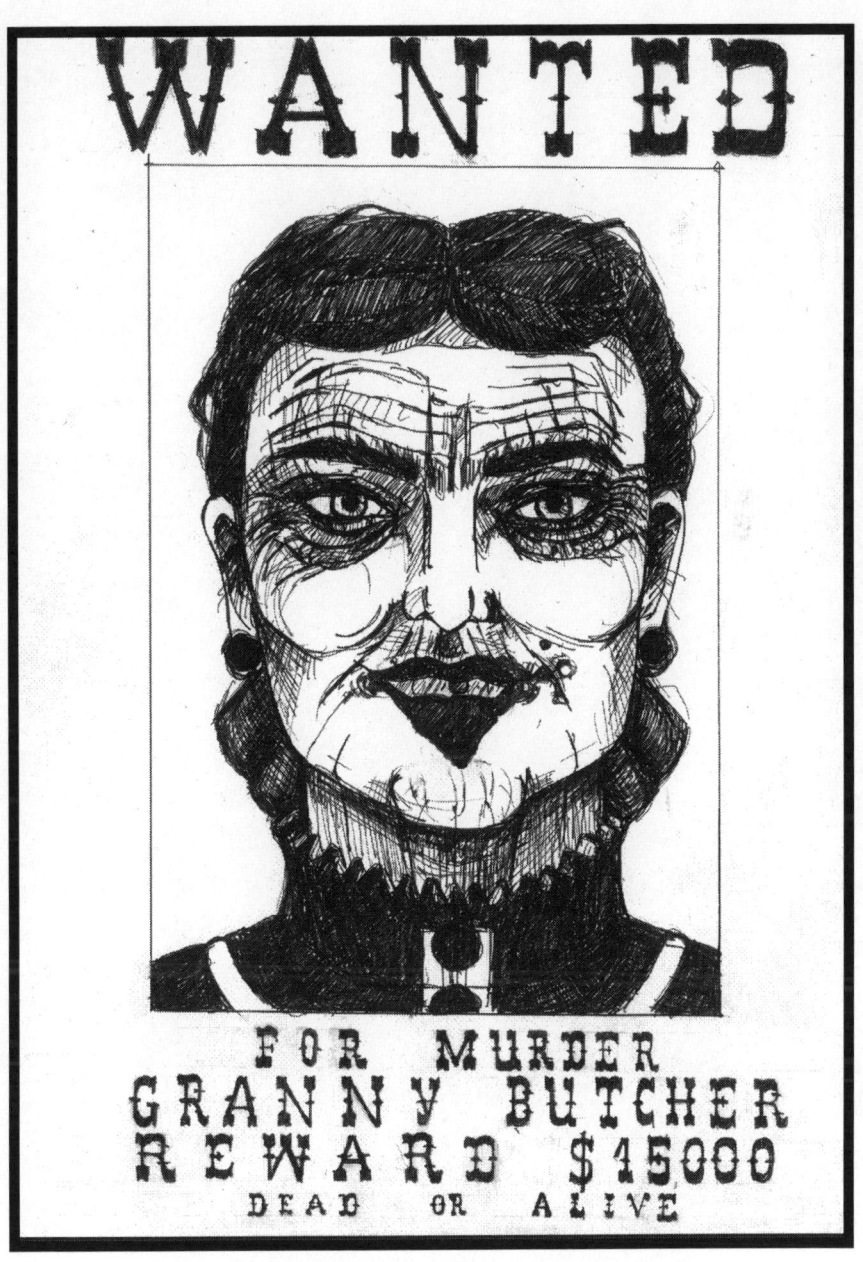

Horror and halitosis – *here comes Granny!*

The Wrath of Skull Creek

***A tale known to some folk as
"Randy's Last Stand"***

I left my ranch and Billie-Jo as sunlight kissed the skies,
with Jed, my buddy, at my side and Stan between my thighs.
My Billie-Jo still wanted kids and told me, "While away,
keep usin' the prescription from the doctor twice a day.
They'll help your little swimmers reach my eggs and play the game."
Her sisters bred like desert rats – that's why I took the blame.

Jed was kinda moody as we waved my wife goodbye.
I guess our destination would unnerve the toughest guy.
I knew that Jed both could and would, if chance of romance beckoned,
divest a man of fastened chaps in less than seven seconds.
If he un-holstered both his weapons just as lightnin' fast,
I'd need him if a gunfight started, if I hoped to last.

I felt a deep foreboding as we crossed the desert plains.
My quest for peace of mind would risk a bullet to our brains.
I was just as scared that Skull Creek memories I'd suppressed
would cause some harm if they returned and leave me more distressed.
That town had spawned more villains than the fiery pits of Hell.
I'd married one called Kate who'd stuffed my horse and friends as well.

The deaths of Frank and Jesse, when Kate filled 'em full o' straw,
had festered long inside of Jed and he was out for war.
And even Annie, my ex-wife, once tracked, without a respite,
the Skull Creek killer, Bobby-Ray, a Butcher clan transvestite.
I trekked with Jed in silence till the sky was leakin' red
and paintin' pretty orange hues on canyons straight ahead.

I pitched the tent while broodin' on the certain price of failure,
while Jed unpacked the herbal cure to treat my genitalia.
We lit a fire and fried some beans, then watched the moon arisin'.
The coal-black sky was full o' stars, their beauty still surprisin'.
Our breath left vapour trails, as moonlight danced on every crag,
and while I slept, Jed slyly snuck into my sleepin' bag.

I mumbled as I slumbered. Demons chased me through the night.
Then somethin' sharp awoke me at the crack of mornin' light.
"Whoa! What's that stabbin' in my back?" I said to Jed, and he
replied, "I'm sorry, Randy, but I guess I need to pee."
I noticed, peerin' through the tent-flaps, Stanley's pryin' snout.
He huffed with indignation, thinkin' he was missin' out.

We figured there'd be three more days of roastin' desert trail
before we reached that wretched town and devils' holy grail.
Jed reapplied my herbal rub. We mustered our resources,
then set off in the blazin' heat on slightly sulky horses.
We blistered as the days passed by all blurrin' into one,
then Hell was standin' in our path beneath the settin' sun.

We tethered Stan and Ollie to the rail by the saloon,
but Stan reared up and squealed as if he sensed impendin' doom.
I turned to face across the square where Nancy's Inn still stood,
as folk appeared at windows right across the neighbourhood.
I strode with Jed towards the Inn. He went to hold my hand,
but I was tryin' to hide how much it shook on Satan's land.

Half way over, hell broke loose and Jed invoked a prayer,
as every inn, saloon and store spat freaks into the square.
The ladies cussed, all mean and scarred. The men wore mostly dresses,
and Bobby-Ray's survivin' bro had tied his hair in tresses.
Their guns and cattle prods were drawn, and they intended harm,
and in their midst a wizened crone appeared without an arm.

She croaked with wrinkled malice, "Hey, the dancin' boy came back!
You tasted nice at twenty, now I'll get a second crack."
I gasped and felt my hackles rise. Jed's face showed real concern.
I'd swear I'd never seen her, but a memory returned:
Her grandsons were the Butcher boys. They'd lured me to her lair
and held me as she'd stripped my clothes and dropped my underwear.

That's quite a skill with just one arm, but I recalled the truth.
She'd also bared her gums and used her last remainin' tooth.
And then she'd drawn up close and I had sensed her passion grow.
Her stagnant tongue had left her mouth and licked me head to toe.
I'd wriggled as her laughin' boys increased their vice-like grip.
She'd moved her face to mine, a cold sore weepin' on her lip.

Her single tooth had rotted brown, but worse, her stinkin' breath
had launched a cloud of halitosis, lingerin' like death.
Then Bobby-Ray had poked me with a tool grabbed from a bench,
while Granny's tongue had stormed my mouth and started kissin' – French!
The taste was sour, like rancid meat that festered with decay.
Her boys had howled, but dropped their guard–that's how I broke away.

My guns were in their holster on a chair as I flew past
and somehow I had grabbed 'em by the belt while sprintin' fast.
I'd dived towards a window that was shut and locked and round,
and shattered glass preceded my descent towards the ground.
It must have been five storeys high – an attic room at least.
A neon "Nancy" sign flashed by – that's when I saw the priest.

I know I would have died without the pastor passin' thru
as, luckily, he broke my fall, although it killed him too.
I shook my head and found myself back in the "here and now"
where once again a screechin' voice spewed from that lawless cow:
"Your Annie stole my Bobby-Ray, and now I'll steal a kiss.
So pucker up my Randy friend – prepare yourself for bliss!"

I told her, "There's no goddamn way you'll lick my face or ears.
I'd rather kiss my own grandma – and she's been dead for years."
So Granny Butcher spat, "If that's your choice, the loss is yours,
as I'm still known to be the best of all the Skull Creek whores."
She told her people, "Randy's rudely spurned my lovin' habit,
so raise a toast with all your guns. It's time to let 'em have it!"

But Jed stepped right in front of me and said, "Don't hurt my Randy,
as he's the finest friend I've got - and also great eye-candy!"
The sound of hammers bein' cocked and double-barrels loaded
resounded loud on every side, and then the town exploded.
Ol' Granny flew in several pieces right across the square,
the scent of blood and lavender left hangin' in the air.

Behind the place she'd stood, the Inn was swamped in ragin' flames,
and through the smoke, on horseback, came the legend, Annie James.
I glanced at Jed who briefly grinned; surprised we'd both survived.
He looked as stunned as me to see my ex-wife had arrived.
All around us, firin' freaks had faltered in dismay,
then carried on with rage at Granny's death to make us pay.

Jed had killed a few and emptied both his weapons twice
while they were strugglin' with their aim as smoke got in their eyes.
I yelled, "Hey, Annie, you're a guardian angel and delight."
She said, "You'll like my box as well - it's full o' dynamite!"
Then right behind us, Creek saloon belched forth a second blast,
and Jed and I both dived to dodge the debris flyin' past.

The townsfolk dropped their guns and scattered, drenched in blood and beer,
while one nabbed Granny's charcoaled bloomers as a souvenir.
Annie said to me and Jed, "Let's take these bastards down,
and any left alive can fill the slammer in the town".
We tracked the evil ladies and transvestite outlaw men,
and either they surrendered or we executed them.

About a dozen still remained, locked safely in the jail,
though Annie spanked the wretch who asked to be released on bail.
She thought about the big rewards, then shrugged and sighed, "So what!
I've earned enough from Skull Creek villains. Leave 'em here to rot."
Before we left, Jed nipped behind the jail to have a pee.
I thought it odd he used a wall, when most men use a tree.

One time he'd used a cactus – stood too close – and every spine
had made the doctor question why he'd shagged a porcupine.
But as we parted, Annie checked inside her ammo box
and thought some sticks o' dynamite were missin' from her stocks.
A grinnin' Jed got on his horse and caught up mighty fast.
That's when the jail exploded in a thunderous, boomin' blast.

Ridin' outta hell! The fall of Skull Creek?

The shrapnel flew, accompanied by blood and somethin' messy
that hit our backs, as Jed informed us, "That's for Frank and Jesse."
That night we camped together, Annie fuellin' my desire.
We all got drunk and raucous, dancin' naked 'round the fire.
I shared a blissful night with Annie, cuddlin' up till dawn,
though somehow Jed had slipped between us by the early morn'.

Next day, she said she'd little time for romance, tacklin' crime,
so thanked me just for makin' love to her a second time.
I frowned and glanced at Jed, confused, as if I was a dunce.
I'm sure I'd have remembered if we'd made love more than once.
I wandered over to my friend and whispered in his ear.
He said, with all the mayhem, he'd forgotten he was queer.

As Annie waited by the tent to say our last goodbyes,
I shed a tear, then held her tight. I'd miss her soulful eyes.
With Annie gone we trekked for days, then camped a final night.
I woke up feelin' crushed. Why was my sleepin' bag so tight?
I felt behind me. There was Jed. Then Stan brayed in my ear,
which wasn't good, as too much sun had caused him diarrhoea.

Returnin' to my ranch, I smelled a lot like Stan's behind,
but Billie-Jo was pleased to see me, actin' awful kind.
A year passed by until a package landed at my door
that kicked and wriggled, with a note that said: "The kid is yours.
He needs more love than I can give while hunting wanted men.
So please look after Joshua until he's nine or ten."

The little fella laughed, so I picked up my son and heir,
who swiftly screamed, then peed on me, and yakked up in my hair.
I guess my doctor's herbal cure for infertility
had worked its magic after all, and saved the family tree.
And though my Billie-Jo was still unable to conceive,
she loved that nipper like the finest gift that she'd received.

We'd often let Jed baby-sit and Josh would seem beguiled,
and somethin' looked quite similar about the way they smiled.
I raised my boy to be a wrangler on the red terrain,
while Skull Creek fell – a ruined wreck that never rose again.
Yet some folk claimed, when desert winds blew over from that way,
they heard ol' Granny Butcher screechin' threats with Bobby-Ray.

"Heck! Why's my sleepin' bag so tight?"

Epilogue

Written by Randall J. Jackson at the Last Chance Saloon care home, shortly before a sponge bath from nurse Kelly, 25 March 2011.

My English editor, Stuart Lee Groom, asked me for an "epitaph" for this poetry collection. I think he meant to say "epilogue", but hadn't really expected me to be alive by the time the book was ready for publication. He sure is a queer ol' fella, with his quaint accent and dandy ways. Anyhow, I ain't one to turn down the chance of havin' the last word.

A lot's happened in the last year. Sadly, my Billie-Jo passed away six months ago, and I've moved into a retirement home myself. I was feelin' a lotta grief for a few months after she died, but at my age you can't afford to spend too much time feelin' sorry for yourself. I've always believed in makin' the most o' life and now, with the Grim Reaper breathin' down my neck, I'm determined to make a real nuisance of myself for as long as I can.

Annie James, the big love of my life, has also been gone a few years now. I'll never forget her arrivin' on horseback at Skull Creek with enough dynamite to blow a big hole in the entire State of Arizona. Of course, since then, our race has developed a real talent for blastin' things to smithereens, from Hiroshima to the Twin Towers and right down to every other suicide and terrorist bombin' of modern times. How those bombin' bastards justify all that killin'n'maimin' in their retarded, godforsaken minds sure beats the hell outta me. Some days it makes me feel ashamed to be human.

On a happier note and by a strange coincidence, Jed was already lodgin' in the bedroom next-door at the Last Chance Saloon care home when I got here. I guess there's no good reason why he should still be alive and breathin' today, as he's almost as old as I am. But in truth, the reason

I think he's thrived is that he's always stayed true to himself his whole life. He ain't never tried to be somethin' he wasn't just to fit in or be liked. In my opinion, that's the only recipe you need for rude health and longevity.

I lost touch with Jed for a long time around about 1961, while he was still in his late fifties. He found the "True West" that his heart had always longed for, when he moved to San Francisco, just as Flower Power was takin' off and free love was available to anythin' that had a pulse. He stayed there for more than twenty years and settled down with a fella called Ralph who, at forty-five years of age, was kind of a toyboy lover. Jed was still handsome back then and he keeps a picture of himself and Ralph on his dressin' table, which shows the two of 'em standin' arm in arm with The Village People. I'm sure he told me that Ralph took the place of The Village People's regular "cowboy character" on a tour once, after the poor guy had been injured by a flyin' studded jockstrap that was flung at him by a male admirer at an earlier concert.

Sadly, the '80s brought that dreadful plague to town and Ralph took ill early on. Jed came back to Arizona alone, all broken apart in spirit. Then Casey came along and they built their own ranch and a new life together. And that's quite an achievement when you're in your seventies. I was pleased for the pair of 'em, as I think that anythin' based on true love is a commitment worth celebratin'.

As for me, I'm gonna die with my chaps on. And probably nothin' else! And they're ladies' chaps, as I'm sure you recall, which I always found suited me better. They're tighter than men's chaps and show the full effect of my brawny thighs, makin' me an irresistible miracle of temptation to anythin' in a bra. I just can't get over myself some days!

In fact, when I stand next to Jed, shavin' in the mornin' at the bathroom mirrors, even he tries to get into my chaps from time to time. But his arthritis is as bad as his eyesight, and I don't think he's got a hope in hell of unbucklin' those straps in a month o' Sundays. Last time he tried to, he didn't realise that he'd actually spent an hour unlaggin' the pipes in the bathroom.

Anyhow, my son, Josh, should be visitin' later. It's funny but, every time I look into his eyes, I'd swear he's the spittin' image of Jed. And I don't think that's the only thing they've got in common.

I'm actually fine about bein' here at the Last Chance Saloon care home. All the care assistants are pretty young ladies and one of them's promised me a proper bath later, so I don't have too much time to spend gassin' away to you folks. And I reckon I've still got enough strength to pull nurse Kelly into the bath with me. I'll tell you – her eyes really sparkle when she sees me. And I feel a sparkle too.

I always used to say that young people ain't just for makin' love to. What a ridiculous notion that was! Of course they are! They won't stay young and pretty forever, and oughtta be grabbin' everythin' they can *while* they can. And though it's said that youth is wasted on the young, it sure as hell ain't wasted on me. In fact, it's perkin' this ol' fella up no end.

Nurse Kelly's just walked into the room – with a big smile on her face and a giant bath sponge in her hand. So I'm gonna have to sign off.

Maybe that English editor of mine was right all along. Perhaps I am dead, 'cause right now, surrounded by all these pretty young care assistants, I feel like I'm twenty-two again and standin' at heaven's door. So, Stuart, if it's an epitaph you want, let it be:

**Here lies Randy Jackson –
hot, horny, covered in soap suds and
mighty happy to be fumblin' around in paradise.**

The End...?

Bonus Feature:

An Editor's Tale

A Letter from Stuart L. Groom to his Family and Friends

"I feel kinda sorry for my English editor, so I've let him include this piece in my collection. It ain't anywhere near as good as my writin' but it's okay…"

- **Randall J. Jackson**

Annus

A gay and festive "Hiya!" to all of you, as we reach the end of what has been a packed year for my Colombian partner, Carlos and me.

We began the year in an unusually adventurous fashion, parascending over the mangrove swamps of Guatemala. Unfortunately, the towline from the speedboat snapped and the canopy tore away, causing me to drop from the skies like a dead bird. Carlos said, in what I felt was an unkind dig at my ever-increasing weight, that my fluorescent red safety vest made me look like a bloated, round robin plummeting towards the festering swamp.

While I was lucky not to be hurt more seriously, I did need surgery to remove a firmly lodged Red Mangrove fruit, which has a sharp-pointed root that develops while still on the branch. It took a further month for my startled expression to fade.

February brought the fiercest winter for several years with deep snow and ice (but I'm sure you all remember that!). For several days, the roads were impassable and supermarkets were closed, as supplies could not reach them. For three nights in a row we had Cup-A-Soup for tea.

Spring brought sad news when great aunt Bettie died in a road traffic accident. Still, she'd had a good innings and, to be fair, we had warned her frequently to exercise caution while skateboarding on the motorway.

We visited my sister and her family one weekend in April. It was lovely to catch up, although her son is now a hoodie teenager. I wandered into the kitchen while he was at the cutlery drawer. I must have startled him as he turned around brandishing a vegetable-peeler in what I felt was a distinctly threatening manner. I am ashamed to admit it but my bladder spontaneously released. I had no spare clothes and had to borrow an outfit from my niece, which was surprisingly slinky and really suited me. The experience was an epiphany that changed me at a deep level. I immediately gave up my job as a publishing editor and spent the whole of May designing ladies' fashion wear for my *Mince Joyeuse* label, finally unveiling my summer collection on the Parisian catwalks at the beginning of June.

Carlos joined me in Paris for a break after the launch and I was especially glad for an opportunity to practise my French, although Carlos thought I was showing off. I didn't understand why the lady behind a supermarket delicatessen slapped me so hard, but Carlos thought I'd used an incorrect word. She then grabbed me by the lapels and dragged me across the counter towards her *visage terrible*.

I was escorted from the *supermarché* by two burly security guards, with a marinated *escargot* embedded deeply in each nostril. I could smell nothing but garlic butter until the end of summer.

I've since found out what I actually said to the *vendeuse*, but I'll spare your blushes, as I'd hate to be accused of inappropriately sharing *too much information!* One should always know exactly where to draw the line.

July is the month when Carlos and I celebrate our anniversary and, this year, we decided to celebrate our commitment with mutual genital piercings. We invited family and friends to a lovely little ceremony, where the Prince Albert commitment rings were skewered into place. My two toughest uncles fainted. However, my mum – perfect for the job as a keen blood sports enthusiast – took some fantastic photos on her new digital camera.

I seem to have skipped Carlos's birthday in early June, but we couldn't do anything very exciting due to my fashion launch and the strict terms of his antisocial behaviour order, which expired just afterwards. His fiery Colombian temperament had landed us both in trouble earlier in the year during the final of an amateur ballroom dancing contest, *Strictly Come Prancing*. Carlos takes his dancing very seriously and felt that I'd sabotaged our chances in the *Paso Doble* by getting drunk the previous night, as it requires great concentration and coordination. Anyway, in a fit of pique, he swung me too hard on the dance floor, inadvertently flinging me into the sixth row of the audience and injuring several spectators. The magistrate has also banned him from ballroom dancing for the next three years.

In August, Carlos returned to Colombia to visit his family, so I seized the chance to join a men's retreat in Scotland, as a birthday present to myself. It was a themed event that aimed to reconnect each of us to our inner *shamanistic warrior prince*. However, I discovered my inner princess instead, although, on Carlos's return, he informed me that I'd been in touch with it for quite a while. He told me that if I didn't "butch up my act" he'd leave me for someone more masculine. I flounced around the flat in high heels, slamming doors and angrily swinging my handbag before calming down. He had a point, I supposed.

In September, to avoid losing Carlos, I leafed through the "groups and local interests" section of the local newspapers, looking for manly pursuits. I decided to join a rugby club that was advertising for new members, to foster my burgeoning machismo. I scored a conversion at my first match – his name was Duncan, a tighthead prop to my hooker. Duncan was recently married but confused about his sexuality. Apparently he was so agitated at his wedding that he turned and kissed the best man instead of his bride. Duncan is no longer confused.

In October, I became vegetarian after an evening with Carlos at a gourmet fish restaurant, when I ordered *lobster thermidor*. The waiter brought a bucket of water containing four live lobsters to the table and asked me to choose between Sidney, Tiffany, Brett and Britney. He had tears in his eyes and sobbed as he informed us that he'd already lost Cheryl, Danni, Simon and Louis to the boiling cauldron on the kitchen stove. Carlos got up and gave the distraught waiter a hug.

We subsequently heard that the waiter had been sacked after forming a similar emotional attachment to a bucket full of prawns that he had also named individually. The final straw came during a lunchtime shift when the waiter snatched back a half-eaten prawn sandwich from the hands of a brunching diner, tearfully proclaiming that he would give it a decent burial that befitted the brave corpses of his cherished companions.

Of course, my health suffered badly during the month of November. I think it was mainly due to the recent change of diet, which brought on regular bouts of diarrhoea and the most frightful stomach cramps. A local artist was able to incorporate my surplus stool samples (originally intended for medical analysis) within his modern art piece, "Full Of It", which is currently on display at the Round Robin Gallery. Needless to say, it was a month I was very glad to see the back of.

December brought early snowfall in the Alps, which also heralded an unusually early start to the winter skiing season, which Carlos and I were able to take advantage of. However, continuing heavy snowfall often meant skiing in whiteout conditions.

On our fourth morning, as we took the chairlift to the top of the mountain, I thought that poor old Carlos must be feeling utterly frozen. He doesn't always wear underpants (a personal thing rather than a Colombian thing) and the bitter, howling wind of a driving blizzard accompanied our ascent. I was relieved to reach the summit, eager to get moving again to counteract the cold but, as we alighted the chairlift, it became clear that Carlos also hadn't properly zipped up the front of his salopettes. Unbeknownst to him, his Prince Albert piercing must have become trapped between the slats on the seat of the chairlift. He rolled forward and was then transported back down the mountain hanging upside-down by his commitment ring from the underside of the chair. As he disappeared into the snowstorm I could still hear his screams, which triggered major avalanches in the neighbouring valleys. Eleven off-piste skiers were swept to their icy deaths in the thundering tidal waves of hurtling snow.

Sensibly for us, we had taken out the platinum ski insurance policy and were flown back to England so that Carlos could receive proper medical care. I shall be visiting him later today and, fortunately, despite the terrible swelling and bruising, he is expected to make a full recovery. And the great news is that the catheter should be out in time for him to come home so we can enjoy a traditional Christmas Day together.

Carlos wanted me to wish all of our friends and family a very Happy Christmas. My mum has taken photos of his wounds, which you can view at her latest lover's website, dick_schotts@lewdster.co.uk. I'd also like to add to Carlos's kind thoughts by wishing you all a prosperous, adventurous and very Happy New Year.

Acknowledgements

My writing aspirations go back a long way, despite following an unrelated career path. Sometimes it's been hard to hold on to my dreams and tempting to find excuses for giving up – *I've left it too late, I don't have enough time, no one will be interested, I might not succeed* – and so on.

There are countless distractions and much easier options than hard work, especially alongside a fulltime day job. Fortunately, the following people helped to keep me on track, and I'd like to express my gratitude to them.

A big *thank you* to my mum (Helen), Martine and Alex for their encouragement and belief in me over the years, including their constructive feedback on Randy's adventures.

Thanks to Jessi for her fabulously madcap illustrations that perfectly capture the essence of Randy's world.

Thanks to Bev, Jeff, Michaela and Simon for their practical support and much more (artist contact, Wild West fonts and images, spotting first draft errors, useful suggestions, etc).

Thanks to the members of Deal Writers for their critique on the poems and pieces that I struggled with the most – especially to Alan, Gary, Jo, Jen and Marilyn.

Thanks to my work colleagues, Dani, Kathy, Lou, Luke and Sarah, for their enthusiasm for Randy from the outset, which spurred me on, and for allowing me to discuss creative ideas with them.

I'd also like to express my gratitude to the men from the Edward Carpenter Community who witnessed Randy's first two stand-up "cabaret" performances and gave overwhelmingly positive responses to both.

Without the generous encouragement, honest feedback, enthusiasm and support of these people, Randy would have remained an unknown ghostly figure, roaming the barren, windswept desert plains of my mind.

Thank you.

Coming to London soon:

The Broadway Spectacular...

RANDY

The Musical

Featuring the smash hit songs –

Happiness is a Half Price Whore

The Cowboy in Me (Jed's Song)

French-kissin' Granny Broke My Heart

Get Outta My Sleepin' Bag, Stanley

&

Sentenced to Hang by Pecker

Backing vocals by the world-renowned
Skull Creek Transvestite Chorus

Printed in Great Britain
by Amazon.co.uk, Ltd.,
Marston Gate.